I0456317

ALASTAIR MAYER

A SAMPLER

Six short stories and a novel excerpt

Mabash Books

First printing, June, 2018
Mabash Books, Centennial, Colorado

Trade Paperback: ISBN-13: 978-1-948188-14-2

CONTENTS

For announcements about other T-Space books and special offers, sign up for Alastair Mayer's mailing list at

http://www.alastairmayer.net/

About the Author

ALASTAIR MAYER'S short stories have appeared in several magazines and anthologies, often enough in *Analog Science Fiction* magazine to gain him entry to the "Analog MAFIA" (Members Appear Frequently In *Analog*). His *T-Space* (terraformed space) series now comprises six novels and several short stories.

Born in London, England, he moved to Canada with his family as a young boy. He describes his interest in space flight and science fiction as genetic: his father, Douglas W.F. Mayer, had been an early member of the British Interplanetary Society as well as a science fiction fan (who in fact published some of Arthur C. Clarke's first tales in *Amateur Science Stories*).

After leaving Queen's University in Kingston, Alastair became involved in both the L5 Society (now the National Space Society) and computers, publishing articles in *Byte*, *Final Frontier*, and other magazines, as well as becoming an accomplished scuba diver and a private pilot. In 1989 he moved to Colorado, where he still lives, and where he works for a satellite network company.

Visit his web site at www.alastairmayer.org.

The Gremlin Gambit

"M'am?" She looked almost young enough to be my daughter, if I'd had one—attractive, slim, barely up to my shoulder. The green hair was odd, especially here, but at least she was in civvies. "Nobody told me I had a visitor, who are you?" She had to belong on the base; this place—Air Force Flight Test Center, also known as Groom Lake, Area 51, and Neverland among others—has the tightest security in the United States. She'd been waiting in my office, green hair and all, when I got back from the briefing.

"I'm here to offer our help against the attackers."

The briefing had been grim. An alien fleet had materialized well within the orbit of Saturn, in the constellation Eridanus. They knocked out half our meager—and secret—space forces and landed heavy hits on Earth before we knew what was happening. "Surprise attack" would be a massive understatement; for all the popular myths about this base, we didn't even know there were alien lifeforms out there.

"You can call me Titania," she said.

The name sounded Russian, but the Russians—and almost everyone else on the planet—were already helping. What was this? Another thought came to me and I made it a joke.

"Titania as in Queen of the Fairies?"

Her eyes flashed. I'd always thought that was just an expression but I'm sure I saw a glint of green. Then she grinned and the room seemed to brighten. "My grandmother, if you must know."

"Ha ha." I thought she was playing along, but this really wasn't the time for jokes.

"Seriously," she said.

Okay, I had a nut case on my hands. I didn't know how she'd gotten in but I reached for the phone to call Security. "Ma'am, I don't have time for this, I'll have to ask you to leave."

She stepped over and pushed the phone down into its cradle, her strength surprising me. She stared down at me.

I'd been sure she was shorter when I first came in, and the green glimmer in her eyes was back. There was a strength here that I found strangely attractive.

A hint of anger edged her voice. "No, *you* listen, Darling."

She wasn't being familiar, that's my name, General Darling.

"*We* don't have time for this. The Earth is our home too. It's in danger. You need our help."

We needed all the help we could get. I still had no idea who she was or what was going on, but she was right. Hell, we all knew Earth was done for if we didn't find some way to resist the Eridani.

"But, but—" I hate when I stammer. "Who *are* you?"

She sighed. "I told you. My name's Titania, and yes, my grandmother is Queen of the Fairies. I'm a fairy."

I choked back my reply.

"What, you were expecting some diminutive Barbie with a minidress, Wilma Flintstone hairdo and dragonfly wings?"

I blushed. "Well, maybe butterfly wings."

"Disney has a lot to answer for. Okay, look, we're wasting time, the second enemy fleet is on its way. If it takes a demonstration. . . ." She did something with her hands and the air around her *sparkled* , like the transporter effect from *Star Trek*, then she faded out and the sparkles condensed to a spot of light which hovered in the air above my desk, like ball lightning. It—she?—darted off and did a quick circuit of the office, buzzed me once, then dispersed into a cloud of sparkles again. Titania stood before me. "Convinced?"

I couldn't say anything. My mind kept looping on the audience response in the children's play: "I do believe in fairies, I *do* believe in fairies."

I sat down, digesting this. "Okay, yes, I'm convinced." There was still the Eridani. "How can fairies help?"

"It's not just us fairies. The rest of Earth's magical folk are in the same danger, worse than anything you humans have done." I must have winced at the word "magical," because she paused and then said "Look, if it will make you feel any better, think of it as Arthurian magic."

"Arthurian? Merlin?"

"Leave Great-Granddad out of this. No, silly. As in Arthur C. Clarke. 'Any sufficiently advanced technology is indistinguishable from magic'; Clarke's Third Law."

"Oh." That did make me feel better. "So you just showed me some *very* advanced technology."

She shook her head, her green hair sparkled with rainbow highlights. "No, I just said if it makes you feel better, you can think of it that way."

"Oh." I stopped feeling better.

Titania muttered under her breath. I caught something about "muggle-wumping mundanes." I'd probably been insulted.

I pulled myself together. "All right, Titania. We've got half the space force we had yesterday and smoking holes in the ground where Buenos Aires and Lawrence, Kansas used to be. If you've got something that will help us fight back, I don't care if it's Bigfoot, Rumplestiltskin or the Wicked Witch of the West, let's have it."

"Now you're talking, Peter."

I hoped she'd gotten that from the nameplate on my door. She sat down and leaned across my desk. "Okay, here's what we're proposing. . . ."

Convincing the senior command group was tough. We had to do a few more demonstrations like Titania's, what I called her "Tinkerbell trick." I only called it that *once* in her hearing; I had donkey ears for the rest of the day.

We made spaceships from almost any vehicle that could hold pressure—mostly aircraft, since some of the magic folk didn't like the iron in submarine hulls. I had asked Titania why they couldn't just create ships by magic. She'd given me a dirty look and muttered something about "pumpkins" and "midnight." I didn't press the point.

They lined the ships with oak panels—a legion of dryads are owed Earth's highest honors for what they did to ensure a sufficient supply of oak quickly enough—and loaded barrels of dirt aboard. I didn't and still don't understand the significance of all that, but Titania insisted. The gremlins— Titania said they were a kind of boggart, whatever that is—didn't care, they *love* technology in their own mischievous way.

"Titania, how are we going to get those ships to the Eridani?" I'd asked when she'd explained the plan.

"Oh, that's the easy part."

"Easy? Even if we could lift them all to space, we'll need a faster than light drive to get to their homeworld. Until they showed up, all our scientists thought that was impossible. Half still do. We still don't have any idea how to do it."

She grinned at me, flashed green eyes, and winked. "Magic, of course."

"What, you wave your—" she didn't have a wand, "hands and poof, the ships are there?"

"No, silly. Fairy dust. We sprinkle it over and through the ships, and they'll fly. And yes, magic will let you go faster than light."

"I thought it was called pixie dust?"

Titania scowled. "That's *another* thing Disney has to answer for. Pixies don't fly."

I changed the subject.

Later, we had two physicists trying to figure out fairy dust, investigating its quantum properties and so on. Bad idea. One ran off to live as a hermit, the other ended up in an asylum, stark raving bonkers.

The plan was simple. We couldn't hope to win in a frontal assault, and if the Eridani realized we were mounting that level of defense, they'd pull out all the stops and carpet bomb Earth with dinosaur-killers. The Faerie, though, are masters of the hidden, the subtle, and the devastating. It's fortunate for humans that they usually keep it amongst themselves.

There'd be a two-pronged counter-attack. Our conventional space forces would put up what resistance they could, with the enemy's gunners and navigators confused by fairy misdirection and will o' the wisps. Then there were the gremlins.

My first meeting with a gremlin had been in my office. Titania introduced us: "This is the head gremlin, call him Murphy."

"That's a joke, right? The gremlin's name is Murphy?"

"No, you couldn't pronounce his real name. *I* can't even pronounce it, so call him Murphy."

I looked at Murphy, who already had my desktop computer half disassembled. "So what *is* your real name?" I asked.

He told me. Titania was right, I couldn't pronounce it, or even imagine how to spell it. Then Murphy grinned and stuck out his forked tongue. So *that's* how he'd made that sound.

"I'd expected someone, well, furrier," I said.

They both scowled at me.

"Oh. Disney again?"

Titania shook her head. "Spielberg."

We discussed battle plans while Murphy absent-mindedly tinkered with my computer. The gremlins

would be our behind-the-lines commandos and sabo-
teurs. They'd wreak havoc with enemy control and
communication systems. Things would go so wrong
as to make our Murphy's Law look like a rarely-hon-
ored custom, yet the damage would seem entirely ac-
cidental, unfortunate, and most certainly not the result of enemy action.

Murphy finished with my computer and reassem-
bled it.

I gestured at it. "That's been flaky lately. Did you
chase your buddies out, will it work better now?"

He smiled and shook his head. "Sorry, that's not
us, that's just Windows."

The plans worked. The second Eridani fleet appeared but soon lost cohesion. Enemy ships wan-
dered off alone to where our defenses could pick
them off, some suffered spontaneous catastrophic
mishaps, and many of their shots went wild. The
third fleet was ragtag when it arrived; by then we already had gremlins in Eridani space. They were en-
joying themselves. There was no fourth fleet.

Later, after Titania and I had welcomed back the
last of our forces as they landed on the dry Groom
Lake lakebed, we stood for a while looking up at the
clear desert night sky.

Titania looked over at me. "I never paid much attention to astronomy, where were the Eridani from?"

"A star called 58 Eridani, about 43 light years
away."

She looked up at the sky again. "Where?" She moved closer to me.

I put one arm around her shoulders and waved the other toward the constellation, toward a loose row of five stars. I pointed, "second star on the right."

"And straight on till morning," she said quietly. It sounded wistful.

"What?"

"Nothing." She sighed. "Sometimes I wish you weren't mortal."

"I've wished that a few times myself. Mostly in combat."

"Oh, Peter, that's not what I meant."

I knew that, but what could I do?

She turned toward me. "This place is misnamed, you know, Neverland."

"Oh?"

She shook her head. "Never mind, I have to go. Goodbye, Peter." Then she kissed me.

I was still catching my breath when she faded into a cloud of sparkles and disappeared.

Snowball

The exploration ship *LifeSeeker* came out of warp again just inside the inner edge of the Oort Cloud. It paused a while, scanning, then made a few short warp jumps in different directions, extending the standard scan to locate planets by their parallax. The crew noted a bright planet within the star's habitable zone—the distance at which water could, though perhaps not would, exist in liquid form—and jumped *LifeSeeker* as close to it as the they dared before continuing in under normalspace thrusters.

"Leader," the Astronomer caught the captain's attention, "this planet has a large moon, but the planet itself is ice-covered. I don't think this could be the origin." He referred to the robotic probe they'd discovered drifting away from this star, inactive but still thermally bright against the cosmic background.

Leader's brow crest flattened in consternation as he considered this. Not the origin? He hated coincidences. "From analysis of cosmic ray damage, you said the probe hadn't been adrift in interstellar space long enough to have come from any other system."

"Yes, Leader. And it was only four percent of the distance to the next nearest star, which is in a very different direction." Astronomer paused. It was unlikely, but—"Perhaps another starfaring race left it?"

"We haven't found any other starfarers yet, or even seen signs. The technology is too primitive, too." Leader made his decision. "Plot course for the moon, and begin an orbital survey on arrival." They could check out the planet itself later; the moon would be easier. Any species who could send a robot out of its solar system could put robots on their moon.

They had indeed. The orbital scans turned up many probable landing or impact sites, locations on the surface showing refined metals and radial dust patterns of low-velocity impact. A hand's worth showed unusual radiation signatures.

"Summary report?" the captain asked the assembled group of science department heads.

"Telescopic analysis shows six sites with structures significantly larger than at any of the others, five of these have nuclear sources in close proximity, all of them have outlying smaller structures or equipment. They are all on the side of the moon facing the planet."

"Interesting. Structures?"

"Octagonal platforms apparently supported on four legs, approximately three bodylengths wide. We located a number of smaller, three-legged structures, one of them near an octagon. We also found several other structures, metal debris from impacts, and possible wheeled vehicles or robots."

"Any signs of activity or possible hazard?"

"None we could detect. No electromagnetic or gravitic emissions beyond normal background, except for the radiation sources earlier noted, and they are low level"

"Very well. Where is the octagon platform that is near a three-legged structure?"

Cartographer brought up a hologram of the moon, made a gesture which caused a number of points on the surface to light in a variety of colors, and pointed to a close pair of lights near the equator, some distance south of a pronounced crater with bright rays. "Here, Leader."

"Ah, nearly at the closest point to the planet. Excellent. We'll land there and deploy survey teams to the other sites. I also want a preliminary survey of the planet. Have a science team take the longboat to do an orbital survey."

"Yes sir. Will they land?"

"Depending on what the survey shows, yes. But no landings without further discussion, and they must stay alert for any signs of activity, organic or robotic."

November 19, 1969—Apollo 12 Lunar Module Intrepid, *descending toward the lunar surface.*

Pete Conrad focused on flying the LM, they were now just four hundred feet above the surface. He'd taken manual control at seven hundred and quickly killed most of their descent speed. He wanted to get close to Surveyor Crater and look around some before kicking up dust. He thought his ground track was a bit too far south. "I've got to get over to the right."

At his side, Alan Bean watched the instruments. "You're at 330 feet, coming down at four feet per second."

"Yeah." He adjusted the controls. This wasn't quite like flying a helicopter; the lower gravity meant the engine didn't use much thrust to balance their weight, which meant he had to tilt the spacecraft a lot more to get the same effective sideways or back-and-forth thrust from it.

"You've got eleven percent fuel. Loads of gas, 300 feet, coming down at five."

"Check."

Bean glanced away from the instruments, looking out the window. "Oh! Look at that crater; right where it's supposed to be! Hey, you're beautiful."

Conrad spared a glance in that direction. That bright object near the rim of the crater, was that Surveyor? But he was still too far north and east.

Bean checked the instruments again. "Ten percent fuel. 257 feet, coming down at five; 240 coming down at five." The LM tilted again as Conrad adjusted course. "Hey, you're really maneuvering around."

"Yeah." He killed the rate of descent some, keeping the craft pitched over to reduce their horizontal speed, he didn't want to overshoot the landing area. There was a spot, between Surveyor Crater and Head Crater. He needed to angle over to it.

"Come on down, Pete."

"Okay."

"Ten percent fuel. 200 feet; coming down at three. You need to come on down." Bean sounded a little nervous, like a passenger trying to press an imaginary brake pedal in a car.

"Okay." Conrad straightened the LM, descending again toward the spot he'd picked out. To the left he could now clearly make out Surveyor III sitting on the gentle slope of the crater where it had landed two-and-a-half years earlier. He focused on the landing; they were getting close.

Bean was intent on the instruments. "190 feet. Come on down. 180 feet; nine percent fuel. You're

looking good. Going to get some dust before long."
In fact Conrad could already see some. "130 feet; 124
feet, Pete. 120 feet, coming down at six. You got nine
percent," the number flipped over, "eight percent.
You're looking okay. ninety-six feet, coming down at
six feet per second. Slow down the descent rate!"

Conrad goosed the control, the exhaust kicked up
more surface dust.

"Eighty feet. Eighty feet, coming down at four.
You're looking good. Seventy feet; looking real good.
Sixty-three feet. sixty feet, coming down at three."

The dust grew thicker outside Conrad's window.
The films of Neil's landing, *Apollo 11*, hadn't shown it
this bad.

"Fifty feet, coming down; watch for the dust."
Bean focused on the displays, not the view out the
window. He hadn't seen the dust yet.

"Yeah." Conrad's answer had a wry note.

"Forty-six feet."

A voice from Ground Control came over the radio. "Low level." That was a fuel warning. Both astronauts glanced at the annunciator panel, the "DES
QTY", descent quantity, lamp was lit. Less than two
minutes of fuel left.

"Okay." Bean started a countdown clock. At
twenty seconds of fuel left, they'd have to make the
decision to either land or abort, jettisoning the descent stage and rocketing back to orbit. He looked
back at the display. "Forty-two feet, coming down at
two. Forty, coming down at two. Looking good; watch
the dust."

Out the window, Conrad could no longer see the
horizon nor indeed much of the ground, so much

dust sprayed out from under the LM. He looked over at the "eight-ball", leveling the spacecraft. But now he couldn't tell if he was drifting sideways or backwards —if he landed with too much horizontal speed, the landing gear could buckle. Even if the LM didn't crash, a bad angle would make it impossible to launch back to orbit. He looked out the window again, managing to see some rocks through the dust that let him judge his speed. He looked back at the eight-ball again to level the ship.

"Thirty-one, thirty-two, thirty feet. Coming down at two, Pete; you got plenty of gas, plenty of gas, babe. Hang in there."

The voice from Houston came again. "Thirty seconds remaining."

"Eighteen feet, coming down at two. He's got it made! Come on in there."

From the side and rear landing legs thin metal probes projected down a few feet below the pads. They touched the surface, buckled. On the LM's instrument panel, a blue, circular light lit up.

Bean saw it immediately. "Contact Light!"

Conrad cut the descent engine, and the *Intrepid* dropped the last few feet to the surface.

LifeSeeker, *near Surveyor Crater*

The *LifeSeeker* was the third spacecraft to land at that spot in the Ocean of Storms. The octagonal platform stood stark near the edge of a gently sloping crater, on whose slope a smaller spacecraft sat on three splayed legs. The *LifeSeeker* survey crew kept a respectful distance, not wishing to disturb the footprints that encircled the octagon and led to the tripod and beyond. A technician suited up and took a gravsled over the site, pausing to take detailed images and scans of the platform, the scattered equipment, and what seemed to be scientific instrument packages, cabled together and in turn connected to a dish antenna pointed up at the planet overhead. The radiation they'd detected came from one of the packages in the instrument cluster, a vertical cylinder with a fins radiating from it. A power source.

"Retrieve the power unit, perhaps we can determine the age from the isotopes," the captain directed. The instruments were long dead, it wouldn't matter.

Other survey teams spread out over the moon in their scoutboats. They found similar instrument packages and dish antennae at five of the sites, a sixth had a simpler experiment suite. Near three of the former they found wheeled vehicles with footprints leading to and from, and wheel tracks leading away in several directions. They followed the tracks and found areas where footprints reappeared, where the surface had been disturbed.

"They must have used the vehicles to cover more distance, then stopped to make detailed studies. Exploring or prospecting." one of the Scouts reported back.

At two other places on the moon they found another kind of wheeled vehicle, apparently entirely robotic, and traced the tracks of each back to landing vehicles.

In many places they found debris, scraps of metal and plastic film and fiber and circuits, smashed and scattered when the original craft had hit the surface at orbital speed or better. They sampled them for later analysis.

* * *

LifeSeeker's *Longboat, near the planet*

The scout team in the *LifeSeeker*'s longboat orbited an almost featureless world. In their careful approach to the planet they'd noted several artificial satellites, some in an equatorial orbit nearly synchronous with the planet's rotation, others in lower, highly inclined orbits. Nobody would deploy so many and such varied satellites around the snowball below them. But they detected no other signs of intelligent life; the satellites' power and maneuvering systems were long dead; the planet's surface almost covered in glaciers. Near the equator there were stretches of open water, and elsewhere in the ice large cracks had repeatedly formed and refrozen. Perhaps an ocean beneath.

"How could intelligent life develop on such a frozen world?" Pilot said.

"Maybe it froze later," Planetologist replied. "This planet is near the outer edge of its sun's habitable zone, near freezing on average. If the sun's output dropped slightly, or the concentration of greenhouse gases fell off too much, or heavy clouds or dust high in the atmosphere blocked the sunlight, that might tilt the balance."

Climatologist picked up the explanation. "Once the ice covered enough of the planet, the albedo would be so high, it would reflect so much sunlight back into space as to cause a runaway feedback cycle and the planet would freeze over. It happened on our homeworld, a billion years ago."

"How did it ever thaw out?"

"Our sun warmed as it aged, volcanic activity increased greenhouse gases in the atmosphere, micro-organisms on the surface of the ice reduced its reflectivity."

"Could that happen here?"

"Possibly. It depends what caused it, what the long term activity of this sun is like, how much tectonic activity there is. Let's ask for permission to land and see what we can determine from ice cores and penetrating radar."

* * *

LifeSeeker, *near Surveyor Crater*

"Physics team, do you have an analysis of the radioactive fuel yet?"

"Partially, Leader. It is primarily uranium-234 oxide, with a significant fraction of plutonium-238 and a scattering of other isotopes, probably decay products. But of more significance is the plutonium. The 238 isotope has a relatively short half-life, about ninety-five years—eighty-eight revolutions of this planet around its sun—and it emits helium nuclei."

"So a useful isotope for a crude power source, then."

"Yes, the generator assembly contained thermo-couples, for turning the heat of decay into electricity. There were similar designs on the probe we found outside this system. But there's something else. The half-life, and the fact that we detected so much pluto-nium with the uranium, means that this couldn't be very old, no more than a few millenia, possibly less. I'll have a more definite number when we've finished the quantitative analysis."

Leader's brow crest bristled in mild surprise. Such a short time? "Get me the number, it might help us figure out what happened."

LifeSeeker's longboat, orbiting the planet

The planetary survey team had part of the an-swer. The first hints had come from a close examina-tion of some of the orbiting satellites.

"This is odd—look at the density of microcraters on the surface of this one," Planetologist said.

"It's probably been up here a long time," Pilot said.

"No, it doesn't correlate with the cosmic ray ex-posure. It's almost like it ran into a cloud of some-thing."

"That could happen, debris from another satellite perhaps, exploded or hit by a meteoroid."

"I'm going to do a trace element analysis on this surface, see if I can determine what hit it, or what it hit."   .

* * *

"It didn't hit satellite debris" Planetologist announced definitively.

"What's your data?" asked Climatologist.

"I'm finding traces of silicates, carbonates, and even chlorides, not what you'd expect from another satellite."

"Salt?"

"Yes, and the silicates and carbonates could be from sea bottom mud. I think a large impactor, an asteroid or comet, must have hit this planet's ocean. The blast would have kicked up the sea floor, the salt would be left when the water boiled away."

"And this satellite flew through the cloud?" asked Pilot.

"I don't have a better explanation."

Pilot just wiggled his brow crest, a shrug.

"I'd like to see what we find with our core sampling and deep radar," said Climatologist.

"The density of this planet is high enough that the oceans can't be very deep, just a skin on the surface. Even a modest asteroid or small comet could hit bottom."

LifeSeeker, *near Surveyor Crater*

The octagonal platforms and the surrounding areas proved the most interesting. All had numerous and overlapping impressions in the dust, oval with several ridges through them. At each octagon, near the base of the ladder-like leg, they found curious, stiff fabric bags, L-shaped, with a hard surface along

the bottom of each. The shape and ridges of this surface matched the impressions in the dust.

"If these were monuments, I'd say these bags or
baskets were some kind of offering," said the Studier
of Ancient Peoples. "The numerical significance is interesting."

"How?" asked the Engineer, who had been examining one of the instruments they'd recovered.

"The platforms have eight sides. We found four
of these objects at each site, and two of the large rectangular boxes. Two, four, eight. See the
progression?"

Another put forth: "And the wheeled vehicles:
four wheels, two fabric platforms."

Engineer's brow crest flattened. "Most of our
wheeled vehicles have four wheels, it's a convenient
number by the laws of physics, not numerology. And
many have two seats, for a driver and observer or nav-
igator."

"And the octagons?"

"Again, a convenient shape. Four legs for a landing craft makes sense, better load distribution than
three, lighter than five. At this level of technology"—
chemical propulsion!—"weight would be critical."

"Ah, and the four baskets?"

"Not baskets, bags. Footbags—they left footprints!"

"But why leave the footbags?"

"I can think of two good reasons," said Engineer.
"They are incredibly dusty, they wouldn't want to
bring that inside their ascent vehicle." Analysis of the
blasted upper surfaces of the octagons had made it

apparent that an upper component had rocketed itself away, presumably returning the visitors home. "And again, the weight. The large box structures, and other debris we found scattered around the base, all probably excess weight jettisoned before launch."

"What do you suppose they looked like?"

"No way of knowing for sure. Probably bipedal, if those were footbags, two explorers per lander, given two seats in the vehicle."

"The footprints look consistent with two legs, and there are no tail drag prints," said Studier of Ancient Peoples.

"I don't think those vehicle seats would work with tails."

"They could have had tail stubs, or thin tails they kept down a suit leg."

"And we have no idea how many upper limbs they had, or heads, or what sensory organ clusters."

"We may eventually determine some of that by analyzing their tools. They'd be designed to be easy to use by beings with a given configuration of manipulatory appendages and sense organs. We can run computer models."

August 2, 1971, the Apollo 15 landing site near Hadley Rille

Jim Irwin and Dave Scott were near the end of their third and last excursion on the Moon's surface in nearly as many days. The official timeline had them transferring their samples to the Lunar Module, and parking the rover a short distance away and aligning the antenna. Their personal, unofficial timeline had one more task.

Scott was behind the rover, out of site of the TV camera, when he heard Joe Allen, the CapCom, back on Earth.

"Jim, how are you doing?"

"Oh, fine, Joe," Irwin answered. "Transferred a few bags up to the porch."

"Sounds good." Allen's reply came back.

Dave opened a bag and carefully removed a small plaque and a polished metal figurine. The crew had planned this in advance, a memorial to astronauts and cosmonauts who had died in the furtherance of space exploration.

Irwin's voice came over the radio again. "We have about three more bags to transfer up."

Allen's response came a few seconds later. "Super." There was a long pause. "And, Dave, you might want to check TV Remote."

He was busy setting up the memorial. "Okay, Joe. Just a sec." Bending down against the pressure of his suit, he placed the plaque standing up on edge, pushed down into the soil a bit to hold it. Then he laid the figurine—a stylized astronaut—face down on the lunar dust in front of the plaque. He looked at the names on the list, he'd known many of them. Authorized or not, this was right. Some of these guys never got to go.

Scott rose, the suit's pressure almost pushing him up. He started to ready the Hasselblad camera to photograph the memorial.

Allen's voice came again over his headset. "Dave, give me a call on your present activity."

"Oh, just cleaning up the back of the Rover, here, a little, Joe." Scott answered. He quickly took a couple of pictures.

"Oh, okay." A pause. If that had sounded as weak to Allen as it had to Scott, he didn't mention it. "And, Dave, we do not have our TV yet. You might want to check TV Remote."

"Okay, Joe."

LifeSeeker, *near Surveyor Crater*

"Just a moment," Studier of Ancient Peoples said, entering some commands to bring up an image on the display over the table. "Look at this, we found it near site five. It doesn't seem to be a tool."

The display showed a metal object lying on the lunar dust, smooth-surfaced and showing little detail, roughly rectangular with a narrow wedge cut out of one end, splitting the object for nearly half its length. A smaller, rounded rectangle protruded from one side just beyond the slot, and the end had a small rounded projection centered on it; the sides of the object, and the projection on the end, were straighter, forming a right angle to the top surface. Near this object stood a larger, thin flat metal plate with row of markings on it. The patterns of markings were similar to markings they'd seen on other equipment, probably a written language of some kind.

"Do you suppose this could be a model of one of them, like a doll or effigy? If it were stood up on the two ends of this bifurcation. . ."

"That would put the smaller knob on top—a convenient spot for a visual sensory cluster. But it has no manipulative appendages, no arms or tentacles."

"It's stylized, or perhaps they extrude from the body."

"In a space suit?" he inclined his head no.

LifeSeeker's *longboat, on the planet*

Radar analysis of the planet from orbit had revealed an important clue. The outlines of landmasses under the ice bore a resemblance to the odd shapes which had been inscribed in circles on the plaques found on the legs of several of the octagons. Those circles must have been representations of the beings' home planet. The shapes were only an approximate match, which caused some confusion until Climatologist reminded them to account for a drop in the ocean levels as ice accumulated on land. Adjusting for that, the match was nearly exact. More evidence that the moon explorers had come from this planet, and it had frozen over since.

The longboat settled on its landing gear on a smooth plain of ice, near the original shoreline in the equatorial zone.

"Are you sure we're on the landward side of the original ocean level?" Planetologist asked Pilot. "We want what would have been dry land when the glaciation started, not ocean sediments."

"If your estimates are correct, then so is our position. But I can move further inland if you wish."

"That won't be necessary." He turned to help Drill Technician with his suit. Once sealed up, they airlocked out onto the icy surface and prepared to set up the equipment a few hands of arms away from the ship.

A strong wind whistled down the icefield from the interior of the continent, picking up flakes of snow and ice, making the air sparkle sometimes under the nearly cloudless sky.

"This is frustrating," said Drill Technician, fumbling with the coupling to the laser head in his suit-gloved hands.

"You could take your gloves off, the air is technically breathable," replied Planetologist.

"No thank you, I prefer my skin unfrozen, and I haven't had feathers since childhood." As with most of his species, the downy feathers which helped maintain body heat in infants had molted as he grew. "All right," he said, snapping the last component in place, "we are ready to begin."

They stepped back to a safe distance and fired the drill. As the laser beam bit down into the ice, a plume of steam jetted out of the hole, freezing out as an icy cloud a few bodylengths above them. After a short while, the plume started blowing smoke and dust fragments, and it hit bottom. The laser cut off.

"How does the data look?" As the beam had been burning its way through the ice, sensitive instruments had been staring down its length and observing the plume. Variations in composition were analyzed. A complete stratigraphy of the borehole had already been recorded before the laser shut off.

"Very good," Planetologist answered, pulling data from the drill's computer to his helmet's screen display. "Look, we have banding, probably seasonal variations." He touched some controls, running another analysis. "A count of 729 cycles, 729 of this planet's years," he said.

"How many of ours?"

"About 787, but that's not allowing for whatever has worn off the top or melted out from the bottom, of course."

"On to the next location," said Drill Technician resignedly. He began packing up the gear.

* * *

February 6, 1971 - Apollo 14 landing site, Fra Mauro Base

Al Shepard and Ed Mitchell were near the end of their second and last walk on the Moon. As they discussed which pieces of equipment would be returned, and which would remain behind to save launch weight, Al picked up the handle of the rake-like contingency sample scoop, pulled a small metal object from a large pocket on the outside of his suit, and began assembling them.

Mitchell was gathering film magazines together, there was one he didn't think had been used. He called down to the CapCom in Houston. "Fred, magazine KK has never been used, is that right?"

"Stand by."

Alan took the opportunity, and stepped in front of the TV camera, holding up the modified tool. "Houston, while you're looking that up, you might recognize the handle of what I have in my hand. It just so happens to have a genuine six iron on the bottom of it." He held something up in his other hand. "In my left hand, I have a little white pellet, familiar to millions of Americans. I'll drop it down." The small ball dropped slowly to the dusty surface. He raised the makeshift club in his right hand, as best as the pressurized suit would allow. "The suit is so stiff, I can't do this with two hands, but I'm going to try a little sand-trap shot here."

The first swing struck the lunar soil short of the ball. Mitchell, looking on, said in an amused tone "You got more dirt than ball that time."

Shepard grinned to himself and acknowledged it. First golf swing on the Moon, and just dirt. "Here we go again," he said, and swung. This time he connected, barely, and ball went off at an angle a few feet.

Fred Haise's voice came over the radio. "Looks like you sliced it, Al."

But Shepard was getting the hang of it now. He stepped up to the ball again. "Here we go. Straight as a die; one more." The swing connected and the ball went off at a low angle, hard to see against the bright lunar surface. Twenty yards? He had one more ball, he could do better. He dropped the second ball and stepped over to it. This was it. He reached back, twisting and raising his arm as much as the suit would allow, and swung. The impact felt solid. The ball soared, a tiny white speck fading into the distance. He grinned. "Miles and miles and miles."

LifeSeeker, *near Surveyor Crater*

The Leader summoned his department heads together in the upper deck briefing room for an analysis of what they'd found., the snowball planet shining in half-phase through the overhead window.

"Physics? Your analysis of the radioactive fuel?" That would give the most definitive dating.

"The composition is consistent with the sample being originally nearly pure plutonium-238 oxide approximately 10.4 half-lives ago," said Physicist, "decaying primarily to uranium-234 oxide."

"Ten-point-four half-lives, making it?"

"About 988 years, or 915 of this planet's years old."

"Nearly a thousand years," the Leader's voice trailed off, thoughtful. "They were landing on their moon when we were inventing steam engines." He pondered this a moment. What were the odds of the civilizations of two different stars developing the same technology almost simultaneously? No, that was premature, he knew little about their overall technology, nor how long it took them to get to this point. "What else?"

Physicist showed images of a flat, square slab, it's surface an array of hundreds of circles. He zoomed the image to reveal those to be a clear solid—sapphire, quartz, diamond, it wasn't obvious which—with the back surface of each cut to a perfect cube corner. "These are retro-reflectors, they will return a light beam back in the same direction from which it came."

"Oriented to face the planet?"

"Exactly. We believe their function was either to provide some way to precisely fix the position of the landing site, or perhaps to allow extremely accurate measurements of the planet-moon distance. Either way you would need a beam of coherent light to reduce dispersion."

"A laser?"

"Precisely."

"So, they had lasers, nuclear reactors, chemical rockets—surely nuclear rockets couldn't be far behind. What else?"

"We disassembled some of the instrumentation," he gestured to a side table where various pieces of retrieved equipment, objects and samples were arrayed. "It's electronic, at a relatively primitive state, but they had semiconductor technology and what we examined was structured in a way that shows they understood the underlying concepts, even if their fabrication techniques were crude."

"Implications?"

"They had lasers, semiconductors and controlled nuclear reactions. But we found no evidence of gravitics—oh there's what was a crude gravimeter, essentially weights on springs, but nothing comparable to their electronics."

"Still, whatever took them out must have happened quickly, almost as soon as they developed space travel." Leader didn't like the implications, it was too coincidental. Was there some outside force involved?

The Planetologist spoke up. "No, Leader, it did not. Our surveys of the ice don't agree with that."

"Oh?"

"We cored down to rock surface, and counted seasonal layers. On average there were only 730, plus or minus a few. 730 revolutions of this planet, around 788 of our years. The glaciation happened nearly 200 years after the moon exploration."

"Perhaps it stopped snowing a while back."

Climatologist joined in. "No, the planet isn't completely frozen over. There are areas near the equator where there's open water, enough to allow precipitation, although much less than when this started. We also ran climate models—tricky, since we don't know the exact starting conditions. The pictures on the plaques helped, giving us an idea of the sea level then, which lowered with the growth of the glaciers."

Another member of the planetary survey team spoke up. "We also found some satellites in high orbit which don't seem to be as old as what was left here on the moon. We don't know the exact cosmic ray flux here over the years, but the orbits were high enough that the planet's magnetic field wouldn't shield them much. The exposure rate would be similar to the rate here. We found satellites of different ages, some as old as the lunar gear, validating our method, and some as young as the probable onset of glaciation. Nothing more recent."

"And the glaciation? What caused it?"

"Impact winter," said Planetologist. "Things must have been near the tipping point, but a large meteor struck and threw up a huge cloud of debris, probably also starting global fires and raising intense smoke. That would block the sun, cooling the planet. Huge amounts of vaporized water would form clouds doing the same, and where that water fell as snow, the ice would build up. If the initial impact is sufficiently catastrophic, even a technological civilization, at least at the level we've seen, couldn't cope."

"But that was two hundred years later. They had nuclear power. Space travel. They must have known how to build nuclear rockets. They had lasers. They were bold enough to send six vehicles and however many robots to this moon, and sent robots beyond their system. Look at where we are," he gestured to indicate the landing site, "they could do pinpoint landings!" Leader stood up and started pacing. This was disturbing. "And they had two hundred years to improve their technology before the asteroid hit. We were starting to build *starships* by then! How does a spacefaring society let itself get wiped out by an asteroid?"

"Perhaps. . ."

"Yes?"

"Perhaps they weren't really spacefaring. If this was a stunt, a single expedition?"

"So much effort? And then throw it away? But they had the technology. Six landings, they had the desire. They had the knowledge—they must have known of the dangers of asteroids, all they had to do is look up at the craters on this moon to see that. No, we must be missing something. What sane species develops a capability and then ignores it?" The captain's brow crest rippled with agitation.

Nobody had an answer. The Leader paced, pausing by the sample table, looking vainly at the artifacts for an answer, but there was none.

A small white sphere caught his eye. He picked it up, examining it. The surface of the white sphere was covered with small dimples, like little craters. Part of the white plastic covering was discolored, almost tanned, probably from the solar wind.

"What's this?"

"We're not sure, sir. We found it some distance from octagon three, the one with the two-wheeled cart. It was a chance find, there were no footprints or tracks leading up to it."

"Curious." He held the ball out at arm's length, then looked out the topside window at the planet overhead, itself a white sphere. In his hand, the small dimpled ball looked the same size as the planet, and nearly as white.

His brow crest flattened. He shook his head and dropped the ball back on the table. He hated coincidences.

Light Conversation

I almost missed it. If I'd looked away as I closed the refrigerator door, I would have. But the light didn't go out. Poly explained later that they (he? it?) had shorted out the switch (at some personal sacrifice) to keep it on, but I'm getting ahead of myself.

People joke about whether the refrigerator light really goes out when the door closes. If you look, though, you'll see it turn off just before that, when the door pushes the switch in. But this time it didn't. I'd been getting a late-night snack, didn't bother turning on the main kitchen light, and the refrigerator light stayed on right up until the door seal hit the frame.

"That's odd," I said to myself, aloud. I do that. I opened and closed the door again, watching closely. The light stayed on.

I didn't *know* that the closed refrigerator was still illuminated, any more than Schrödinger knew if his cat was alive or dead, but a half-dozen schemes to decide came to mind. If I could find my meter I could check the current draw, but I'd have to drag the fridge away from the outlet. There was enough shelf space between the milk carton, the pickle and jam jars, and yesterday's leftovers to put my camcorder, but the battery wasn't charged. Out in the garage I excavated the weed whacker and unreeled a foot of monofilament from the business end. Now I had a crude fiber-optic cable. I closed the refrigerator door on the nylon line, one end protruding. The tip glowed; the light was still on.

I opened the door and squatted down to examine the switch. I pushed it a few times to no effect. I didn't want to commit appliance repair at this hour, but neither did I want to leave the light on all night. As I reached in to unscrew the bulb, I saw Poly.

My first reaction to the yellow-green slime growing on the fridge wall was to recoil in surprise and disgust. I've heard of weird things growing in the back of the refrigerator, but *this*! Resigning myself to the cleanup job, I moved the big pickle jar aside then went to get a sponge and disinfectant spray.

Back at the fridge, I noticed that the slime mold— it resembled chartreuse pudding—now had a raised pattern on its surface. I knew a little about slime molds, that they can move and change shape, but I'd never heard of one creating on itself the diagonally barred circle, Ø, that usually means NO. "Odd" I said to myself again. And yes, again aloud.

I started to reach in with the sponge, and the slime rippled and changed as I watched. I hadn't thought they could move that fast, and was even more surprised when the surface formed, in raised ridges, the letter N. It held that for a few seconds then morphed to show the letter O.

"'No'?"

The slime mold raised two dots and a curve within the O, like this: ☺ . A happy face? Had it heard me?

"Can you hear me?" I must be crazy, I thought, talking to a slime mold.

The mold shaped the letter Y, then E, then S. Then: D, O, N, T, then went flat for a bit, then H, U, R, T, flat, U, S.

"'Don't hurt us'?"

"☺"

"But I only see one of you." A detail like shouldn't have worried me when here I was talking to a slime mold, but I was grasping at the mundane. This was getting decidedly weird.

"C, O, L, L, E, C, T, I, V, E, flat, O, R, G, A, N, I, S, M" it spelled out. It was getting faster.

"You're a collective organism?"

"☺"

"But, what are you? Who are you?"

"*Physarum polycephalum sapiens*" it said. Well, spelled out.

"That's quite a name."

"Don't have name. Intelligent slime mold."

"How about I just call you Poly?"

"☺"

So, I had an intelligent slime mold named Poly in my refrigerator. I had too many questions to know where to begin—most concerning my own sanity. I needed more data.

"Excuse me a moment," I said. Politeness, even to a slime mold, couldn't hurt. "I'll be right back." I headed for my computer.

There was no such thing, according to Google, as "Physarum polycephalum sapiens". There are many kinds of slime molds, organisms with many nuclei in a single blob of protoplasm. Plain *Physarum poly-cephalum* is a yellow slime mold, easy to grow in the lab. It had been the subject of numerous experiments involving intelligence, of a sort. Years ago Dr. Toshiyuki Nakagaki in Nagoya had shown that a slime mold could determine the shortest path in a maze. That might be a chemical tropism rather than "intelligence", but I'm no expert. In 2006, Klaus-Peter Zauner at the University of Southampton built a robot controlled by *Physarum polycephalum*. But that mold—and the robot it controlled—avoided light; why was mine huddled up to the bulb in the fridge? Warmth?

I'd have to ask it.

"4 NRG" Now it was using texting shorthand. I'll translate.

"For energy? Photosynthesis?"

" ☺ "

"How?"

"Absorbed chloroplasts."

It *was* much greener than the web pictures I'd found. That's when I noticed that the salad greens in the vegetable crisper were now salad whites. I'd have to toss those.

"But why are you in the fridge?"

"Need cooling."

That made sense. This communication must take a lot of energy. I didn't know *how* it was intelligent, but I knew that our brains and computers both need considerable cooling. So too must intelligent slime molds.

We chatted in that vein a bit. Poly explained how they (he, it, whatever) had gimmicked the light switch, and assured me that it was reversible.

Slowly I realized that I was missing the big questions.

"Where did you come from?" I asked. "How did you get here? What do you want?"

"Too much philosophy. Want go home."

"Oh." I was tired from the late hour and my mind was numb. In my dazed state I didn't ask where "home" was. Another planet? A parallel world? Dr. Nakagaki's lab?

"How will you do that?"

"Recharge," it began, then "O", "o", ".", "*" followed. This last sequence was animated, not spelled out. The circle shrank to a dot then radiated out and went flat.

"You explode? Disappear? Beam up? What?"

" ☺ "

"But—"

As I watched, the raised circle outlining the face flattened, fading, leaving just the eyes and mouth. Then the eyes went, leaving just the smile. A Cheshire slime mold.

That was more than I could handle. As I closed the refrigerator door I said to Poly: "Okay. But when the last of you leaves, please turn out the light."

Author's Introduction to *Into The Fire*

"Into the Fire" turned out to be my first story of T-Space. It wasn't planned that way, but if you're familiar with the novels, you'll recognize the roots.

Like many stories, the ideas here came from all over:

The core problem came out of an article I originally wrote for (but never submitted to, violating Heinlein's Rule 4 of Writing) *Space Gamer* magazine, on "Alternate Fuel Sources in *Traveller*".

The idea of small, relatively inexpensive starships came from an overheard line at a science fiction convention panel: "what if starships were as common as stationwagons?" (I couldn't bring myself to believe they'd ever be *that* cheap.)

Sawyer's World was named for a girl in my astrophysics class in college. Much later, I wrote an entire novel—*Alpha Centauri: Sawyer's World*—to justify (in world) the name of the planet. (*That* Sawyer is entirely fictional; I just borrowed the last name.)

The overall structure owes a debt to Larry Niven's *Neutron Star*. It makes sense to learn from the best.

There are more Jason Curtis stories in T-Space, only some of them have yet been told.

Into the Fire

The star was the wrong color. I had expected it to be a bright, almost blinding white when I switched on the forward window, but the star off my bow was dull, with a reddish tinge. How had *that* happened?

I checked the instruments; no, not red shift. Odd. Procyon should be bright yellow white, not red. I hailed Procyon Station.

Nothing. I could be as much as a light-hour out, so I didn't expect an immediate reply, but I should have picked up something from one of the beacons. There was no radio chatter at all on the Procyon frequencies, just a ghostly whisper of static.

There was nobody out there. There were two possibilities: one, some disaster had hit Procyon, leaving it red and wiping out everyone in the system, or two, this was the wrong system, and something on the ship had gone wrong.

The odds favored the latter. But what? If I couldn't figure it out and fix it, I was going to die a lonely death out here, wherever here was. It had seemed like such a good idea at the time.

∞ ∞ ∞

The day I got fired I went out to my flying club—aircraft, not spaceships—to fly a few circuits and think about something else. I had one of the club's old rocket-racers—the XCOR, an antique—at the fueling pad and was intent on the liquid oxygen transfer procedure. Condensation flowed around me like cold smoke, making miniature fog banks on the concrete. I could feel the chill through my gloves.

"Well, if it isn't Jason Curtis!" came a voice from behind me. "Hey, Jason, got a light?"

"Menzies, that joke wasn't funny the first dozen times you used it." Greg was an old buddy from the club, who'd gone on to become a commercial pilot. "Where've you been keeping yourself?"

"Off-planet." He said it so casually I figured he meant the Moon or Mars. "So why are you out here in the middle of the day, shouldn't you be working?"

I took a moment to close valves and disconnect the LOX coupling before answering. "I just got fired."

"Say again? I thought you owned the company."

"Part owner. Was. We were bought out a couple of months ago." I stowed and secured the hoses.

"But you said fired?"

"Forced into early retirement. Yeah, look, this isn't the best place to talk." I had to raise my voice at the end, the roar of a plane on the nearby runway drowned me out, emphasizing my point. "I've got the racer ready to go for a few circuits, will you be around?"

"Affirmative, I'll see you in the clubhouse."

Flying the old rocket racer felt good. Technically it's a kind of powered glider; you use the rocket to take off and build speed, then cut the engine and glide to conserve fuel, firing the rocket again when you need a boost. Racing strategy is to find the right trade-off between using the rocket to maintain a high speed, and not using it so much that you run dry and waste time refueling.

I wasn't racing today, and I loved the kick in the back that full throttle gave me. It was tough keeping my airspeed below redline, I wanted to just go and keep going. Ten short minutes later I dead-sticked it back in for a landing and just managed to extend the rollout to the hangar.

Back in the clubhouse I found Greg in the small dining area eating lunch. I joined him and ordered a cola, lots of ice.

"So, Jason," Greg said around a mouthful of fries, "what's this about being fired from your own company?"

"Officially I've 'departed to pursue other interests'. NanoDesign's new owners didn't like my management style."

"You have a management style? I thought you were an engineer."

"Funny." I took a sip of my cola. "Yeah, they originally wanted me to stay on for my expertise, but their approach is to over-analyze before starting anything. I like to just give things a quick pass and then dive in."

Greg chuckled. "Quick pass? Like the time you came back with leaves in your landing gear from a 'quick pass' over some trees?"

"Hey, I pulled up in time, didn't I?" I swiped some fries from Greg's plate; too greasy, as usual. The aging autochef was either long overdue for an overhaul, or the tech liked them that way. "Anyway, a quick pass is the way to succeed in a startup market. The thing is, our new owners are over-cautious; I'd probably have left on my own if we weren't bound by contract."

"But you're out now?"

"Yeah, they even waived the penalty clause and let me keep my share of the buyout money."

"Sounds like a great deal, but you don't look happy about it. Why not?"

"I had to sign a non-compete. I can't work in nanotech for the next five years, and by then I'll be obsolete."

"Ouch." Greg hesitated, as if debating his next words. "So, what did Sharla say?"

"Nothing, we split up a couple of months ago. And no, I'm not looking." Greg had always been trying to fix me up with someone. Come to think of it, he'd introduced me to Sharla.

"Oh, sorry."

"Never mind."

I broke the awkward silence that followed with a new subject. "You know, I was thinking up there in the racer, I need to get away for a while. Maybe I'll buy a sailboat and see the world."

"Sailboat?"

"Yeah, I used to sail. I kind of like the idea of just heading off, setting my own course. It's not like I have anyone to answer to now." I tossed back the rest of my drink.

"I've got a better idea," said Greg. "Buy a starship and see the galaxy."

I almost choked on the ice cubes.

"What!" If I hadn't finished my drink, I'd have spewed it over Greg. "Starship?" Then I remembered his remark about having been off-planet.

"Sure. Well, not the galaxy, obviously, but the nearby stars. Lots of interesting things to see out there, all those terraformed planets. I'm headed out to Procyon—"

"Yeah, yeah." I remembered some of the buzz about terraformed planets, how the first expeditions had found many more Earth-like planets than astronomers had predicted, but I'd been a kid in school and hadn't paid much attention. I'd been more interested in the nano scale. "But *me*, buy a *starship*?"

"Just think of it as a sailboat with a warp drive."

"Come on, starships are huge things. I've seen pictures."

Greg shook his head. "Jason, what kind of planes do we have at the club here? Two-seaters, four-seaters, a couple of single-seaters like that racer you were just up in. What do most people think of when they think of airplanes? Five-hundred seat airliners."

"Oh."

"Exactly. The Alcubierre-Broek equations put an upper limit on how big a warp bubble can be, and the power goes up exponentially with size. Small ships are more efficient. Most of the charters I fly are in the 'sleeps eight' range."

"You fly starship charters? You said you'd been off-planet."

"Yes, shuttling research and exploration teams, some tourist flights. But," Greg returned to his point, "you're a good pilot, if you can handle that rocket racer you can handle a starship. A small one would be in your price range."

"Really?" I doubted that. "How much?"

Greg told me.

"What? That's only a third of what my house cost. How come there aren't more private ships around?"

"Jason, you have expensive tastes. Anyhow, you can get a mortgage on a house. Buying a starship is strictly a cash proposition."

Of course. Life would be tough for a repo man in the starship business.

∞ ∞ ∞

The autopilot was still locked on to the star in front of me, just as I'd lined it up in the guidescope nine days ago. This *had* to be Procyon, even if it was the wrong color. You can't turn a warp bubble. So what had happened?

Whoever said "getting there is half the fun" never went anywhere in a warp bubble. I'd spent the first half-hour staring out at the black lack of scenery, broken only by the occasional sparkle of a dust grain ripping itself apart in the tide at the warp boundary. Finally I admitted that travel between stars really *was* as unspectacular as I'd heard, and turned off the window. The rest of the trip, I'd read and listened to music; I have a large collection of classical rock from last century. Nothing had happened.

It would by nice to talk the problem through with someone, but this was a solo trip. Too bad there's no such thing as faster-than-light radio. A thought struck me and I cued up Klaatu's "Calling Occupants of Interplanetary Craft"—music sometimes helps me think —and pondered the situation.

I was more annoyed than worried at that point. "When all else fails," I muttered, "read the frigging manual." I loaded Dumarest's *Principles of Interstellar Navigation* into the reader, scrolled through the first few pages, and wished I'd picked up something more interactive instead. I kept glancing up at the window.

The silent taunting from my red nemesis made it hard to concentrate. I muttered an expletive, turned up the interior lighting and switched off the window. I looked around the cabin with a critical eye. It was perhaps a bit more lavish than standard but still snug. Bed, eating area, head, everything arranged to make optimum use of space, adaptable to gravity or freefall, a bit like an RV or, yes, a sailboat. With just me aboard I could probably stretch the life support to six months, but it wouldn't be fun. I told the galley to fix me a coffee and floated back to get it.

∞ ∞ ∞

The more I had thought about it, the more I liked the idea. There wasn't anything tying me down. No wife or girlfriend. No job, obviously. If I sold the house I could easily afford a starship with plenty left over, or so I thought.

Greg Menzies had given me a couple of suggestions on what to look for, and the ship I settled on was a mid-size Mitsubishi Sapphire. I liked the lines, a streamlined lifting body capable of a gliding reentry from space. In the simulator, she handled in atmosphere like some planes I'd flown.

Greg had been right, the basic price *was* less than an average house might cost. Then the broker started getting into the details.

"So, will this be just the basic hull and drive package or will you be wanting the optional life-support and avionics?" he'd asked.

"Excuse me?" I couldn't have heard him right. "Life support is an optional extra?"

"Well, Mr. Curtis, some clients want customized installation. Exploration outfits in particular often have specialized requirements—traumapods, decontaminating airlock, things like that—and want to make separate arrangements for that. Of course we're quite prepared to arrange any customization you'd like, or we have several standard packages to choose from."

It went on like that. By the time I'd included the necessary "options" and fitted her out with extra computer gear, comfortable living area, auto-bar, and the custom music system, the price had more than doubled.

The fuel tanks held enough hydrogen to give me a four-parsec—about thirteen light-years—range, or an enormous delta-vee if I used the fusion unit to power thrusters instead of the warp. A warp bubble uses a *lot* of power. One exploration model option is gear to do raw fuel processing, avoiding dependence on commercial hydrogen supplies. I threw that in too.

I named her *Starfire*.

"Jason, how could you *not* call it *Argo*?" Greg said when I told him.

"I'd rather not tempt fate." I've read about my namesake.

With my aircraft pilot's licenses, I only had to pass a test on space traffic regs to get a "no passengers" captain's ticket. I didn't want passengers anyway. I spent a couple of weeks playing tourist in the Solar System, getting used to the ship's handling on thrusters and in atmosphere. At Mars I decided it was time to try the warp drive.

Space Traffic Control frowns on anyone using warp in-system for more than microseconds at a time, and gravity wells make it difficult anyway. Where to go for the first real flight? Sawyer's World, around Alpha Centauri, was already getting more civilized than I wanted; the company that had bought out Nano even had an office there. Greg had said something about Procyon. There was small settlement around Procyon A, that'd be a good first trip for *Starfire*. Maybe I'd run into Greg again.

I got clearance from STC and undocked from the Mars Beanstalk, then moved out to a departure orbit and pointed the ship toward Procyon. I put the guidescope's view on my console and turned on the image amplification to look for asteroids or comets. Even though my path took me out of the plane of the solar system, and even though the odds were beyond minuscule, it would be stupid to run into a rock that I could have seen by looking. There was nothing. I lined up the targeting cross-hair on the bright spot that would be Procyon and let the autopilot bring the ship into exact alignment. When the drive engaged, it would create a pointed bubble— a reverse teardrop— of tortured space that would propel itself, and anything inside, through normal space at about 500 times lightspeed. I pushed the button.

And somehow got myself utterly lost.

∞ ∞ ∞

As I read through *Principles* it dawned on me what I'd done wrong. Or rather, what I hadn't done right. Procyon is one of the brightest stars in that section of sky, seen from the solar system, and I'd lined my guidescope up with the brightest spot on my screen. But I'd set the guidescope to amplify light, and if Procyon had been just out of frame. . . . What I *hadn't* done was confirm that the spectrum of my target matched Procyon's.

Well, I knew where I wasn't. The problem now was to figure out where I was.

I had a way to do that. I brought up the astro-nomical database and ran a query to find all the stars whose spectral type was similar to that of the star out the window. The list began scrolling off the screen. I canceled that, cursed the computer for a stupid machine and added "within five degrees of Procyon as seen from Sol". That scrolled off too, and I jammed down on "CANCEL" again. I added "within four parsecs".

One star matched. BD +5 1668. What kind of name was that?

It was a red dwarf, about three degrees from Procyon. If I'd really missed by *that* much, the guidescope was out of alignment. I'd have to check that. The distance was 3.76 parsecs from Earth. That would make it—I keyed in a calculation—just over a light-year from Procyon, which should be roughly back over my left shoulder.

I swung the ship around. Sure enough, a bright, yellow-white pinpoint burned like a distant arc light. There'd be no missing it this time. With a sigh of relief I settled down to program the autopilot to finish the trip.

That relief shattered when I keyed in the distance. An annoying beep synced to the flashing orange warning message: "INSUFFICIENT FUEL".

Oh, crap.

∞ ∞ ∞

It still wasn't time to panic, although the thought crossed my mind. There was no handy refueling station in this system, but the ship had its own fuel processing gear. I popped up *Starfire*'s manual on the screen.

The ship's fusion fuel was hydrogen, the most common element in the universe. I could extract it from water or ice if I found a source, say a planet or comet nucleus. Alternatively I could use the extensible scoops to skim the atmosphere of a gas giant. Water sounded easier. Back to the astronomical database. I keyed up BD +5 1668, and began reading.

"BD +5 1668. Other names and catalog numbers: Luyten's Star, Gl 273, Hip 36208, —" Okay, skip a bit. "Planets: None. Comments: This star, like many red dwarfs, does not possess a developed planetary system. There are several belts of asteroidal material that never accreted, and there may be an outlying cometary cloud. The existence of the latter is un-confirmed."

"Whaddaya mean, 'Planets: none'!" If it wasn't time to panic, it was beyond time to take things calmly. "How the futz am I supposed to refuel the goddamn ship?" I pushed away from the console and stomped back to the living area to sulk, er, think. Stomping isn't easy in zero-G; the result wasn't satis-fying. I ordered a drink from the autobar.

Somewhere around the third drink, I had the glimmerings of an idea. Of *course* there was hydrogen in this system. It had been staring me in the face. I'd have to do some research; getting it wouldn't be easy. On my way back to the main computer console I told the entertainment system to cue up Pink Floyd's "Set the Controls for the Heart of the Sun."

It was a crazy idea, one I'd have dismissed if I were less desperate or more sober, but it was a chance. Not anything as suicidal as diving at the heart of the sun, or even of BD +5 1668, but maybe I could skim its outer atmosphere.

The *Starfire* could scoop the thick atmosphere of a Jovian planet at orbital speeds; perhaps I could do something similar higher in the star's atmosphere. I didn't need to *fill* the tanks; just ten percent would get me to Procyon.

Again I popped up the astronomical database and the *Starfire*'s manual, and went through the numbers. I'd made too many mistakes lately. I wanted to be sure I got this right.

At first blush things looked good; BD-plus-five-etcetera was a "cool" red dwarf, a mere 3100K—

about 2800C. That was more than normal reentry heating, but much less than the scoops were designed for. Then I worked out flight profiles and realized just how fast I'd be going when I rounded the star.

Oh. I put on Meat Loaf's "Bat Out of Hell".

Of course, "out of" wasn't quite right. I'd be going the other way. If the radiant heat didn't get me the friction heating probably would.

I was going to have to think this through. I grabbed another drink from the autobar and pulled myself back to the cabin area. I left Meat Loaf on as background music.

∞ ∞ ∞

Perhaps the music, or the alcohol, was too conducive to letting my mind wander. I couldn't concentrate on the problem at hand. That didn't bother me, if left alone the subconscious often comes up with better solutions than the conscious, but a nasty, annoying part of my brain kept whispering "you're going to die out here, Jason." The rest of me kept telling it to shut up, buzz off, and let me think.

I thought back on why I was out here in the first place. That last meeting at NanoDesign, I'd accused the new CEO of spending too much time and money planning for contingencies that would never happen, and he had accused me of being too laid back and not taking things seriously. I'd told him that I'd never run into a problem I couldn't think my way out of.

"Until now," that nasty, annoying part of my brain said. "Shut up", I told it, and downed the rest of my drink.

Okay, start thinking. What did BD plus five etc. have going for it? No planets. No confirmed comets. Oh, there must be some out there; they'd be the dickens to find, looking for dirty snowballs in the dark. Radar-absorbing dirty snowballs, at that. What else? Asteroids? What good were they?

I snapped alert. That was it! Asteroids!

This system had asteroids. And I had a plan. Back to the computer.

The music advanced to "Paradise by the Dashboard Light".

∞ ∞ ∞

I was going in. It had taken days to find some likely asteroids. I wanted nickel-irons, not stony chondrites that might blow apart at the wrong moment.

It took over a week to push them into fast sun-grazing orbits. I hated wasting even a little of my precious hydrogen on the fusion thrusters, but you can't push anything with a warp bubble.

The asteroids would be my sunshades. I'd hide in the shadow of one on the way in to the star, then dash out and scoop hydrogen. There'd be a second asteroid passing perihelion for me to duck behind and ride out, again in the shade, to where I could use warp again. That was the plan, anyway.

The computer showed that I might need two passes to collect enough hydrogen for the jump to Procyon. I set up three pairs of asteroids, just in case. Enough of fooling around, I wanted out of there.

My real worry was whether the ship would stand up to the punishment I was going to give it. The stellar data on BD-plus-five weren't precise, and I wondered if a scoop designed for orbital speed through Jovian atmosphere would withstand a faster trajectory through much thinner, but hotter, stellar atmosphere. The calculations said it would, but they were kludged up from what little reference data I had aboard. Too bad the computer didn't have an expert system for hypersonic fluid dynamics.

∞ ∞ ∞

Everything that could be battened down was battened down, and I had reduced internal power to help cold-soak the ship. I drifted in the shadow of the first asteroid—I'd nicknamed it Icarus—as it plummeted starward. Perihelion was in fourteen hours. I thought about jumping away to get some sleep for a few hours, but it would be impossible to get back here; the warp drive isn't that precise, and the local gravity well was only getting deeper. I'd have to trust to the autopilot to keep station with Icarus.

∞ ∞ ∞

An alarm woke me with a start. Okay, only the wakeup alarm. Six hours out now. I wished to hell I had something to do. I checked over my calculations, for the Nth time.

∞ ∞ ∞

Four hours out. The sensors showed that local space curved too much now to risk a warp bubble. I was in for the duration.

∞ ∞ ∞

Two hours out. I'd be making my scoop run soon. I ran yet another radar scan to make sure Daedalus, my outgoing shield asteroid, was on course. I nudged the ship's thrusters to stay in Icarus's shadow. Icarus itself was starting to get hot. It had a slow rotation that I hadn't quite canceled, and as the sun-warmed side rotated into shadow it radiated heat back at me. Still, it was cooler here in its shade than out in the sunlight.

∞ ∞ ∞

Four minutes and counting. The timing wasn't split-second critical; I'd be maneuvering all the way to Daedalus anyway, but I had to leave Icarus before we were too deep in the stellar atmosphere. One more visual check of the cabin: everything secure. I snugged my seatbelts and keyed the checklist one more time.

Scoops: out and locked. Thrusters: idle. Active cooling: on. Hull temperature: 100C. Scoop temperature: 100C. Controls: Free and operating.

Music: "Ride of the Valkyries"? No, I didn't need any distractions.

Okay, here we go. I pitched the nose up and shoved the thrust lever forward. The ship bucked as we left Icarus's slip stream, and the hull and scoop temperatures jumped when the sunlight hit. Clear of the asteroid now, I nudged the ship over and started our screaming rush to where Daedalus should be in twenty minutes. That was about nineteen-and-a-half minutes longer than I liked, but the gas was thin out here.

Perhaps not thin enough. The scoops were heating up much faster than I'd expected, and the hull temperature was already nearly a thousand degrees. I pulled up to climb to thinner atmosphere, feeling the G-forces pull me back and down into my seat as the ship clawed up from freefall. I heard the roaring of the gas—plasma—as it swept past the ship, and the whine of the compressors as the scoops sucked up hydrogen and squeezed it into the tanks. I looked at the scoop temperature: 3500C. Expansion cooling kept the inlet temperature lower, but even that was heating up fast. The cabin was getting warm.

I checked the compressor temperature and was thankful for the hafnium carbide blade coatings.

The hull temperature was still rising, and I pushed the ship higher still. Seven minutes to rendezvous. A yellow warning light lit just as I looked at the compressor temperature again. Damn! I slapped the compressor bypass control to divert the scoops straight overboard; I'd have to settle for what I'd collected so far on this pass. The sounds changed then, the whine of the compressor lowering in pitch and fading, but with new rumbles and vibrations as the outside flow changed.

Still five minutes to reach Daedalus. Sweat dripped off me; the cabin was getting hot but most of that sweat was stress. I caught a faint smell of something acrid but strangely bittersweet. *Burning insulation!* I thought, but I *knew* the electronics were fireproof. Supposedly. I scanned the warning indicators and hunted around for smoke. Nothing. The smell was fading; I hoped I'd imagined it.

I checked the scoop temperature again. It was near redline, and I thought about closing the scoops in mid-flight to stop any further heating. That wasn't recommended, but neither was flying close orbit through a star's atmosphere. If I damaged the scoops without having collected enough hydrogen, I'd be stuck here. I reached for the scoop control. Should I? I checked the temperature again. Still rising, but the rate was slowing. A minute to rendezvous, I should be able to pick up the asteroid soon. I left the scoops alone.

Yes, there it was, leaving a plasma trail that reflected my radar like sheet metal. It was on a skip trajectory; it would bounce off the atmosphere and back into space. I was coming up right behind it. I maneuvered quickly, wanting to get into that shadow. My hull and scoop temperatures were now edging above redline, and the cabin temperature was still climbing.

There was a sudden *BANG!* and the ship rolled and yawed violently to starboard. *Oh crap, now what?* I heaved the stick to the left and goosed the thrusters to push up into Daedalus's wake. The ship responded oddly, and the autostabilizer was blinking a yellow warning light. Yellow, that could be worse.

It was worse; red warning lights started coming on too, and an alarm honked madly. Nothing for it but to keep going. The rock was still hypersonic, so the ride smoothed out when I got into the wake. I worried about that bang. It had been more than just crossing the shock wave. It almost felt like the time I'd hit a seagull while on final approach in an old Cessna. I must have hit a rock chunk ablating off the front of the asteroid. How much damage had it done?

I silenced the alarm and checked the panel again; the starboard rudder actuator still showed a red light, but the autostabilizer light was back to green. The computer had learned to compensate. I breathed a little easier. The temperatures were even starting to drop.

∞ ∞ ∞

It took forever, riding Daedalus's shadow out to cooler space. I listened to the faint crackle and ping of the hull contracting as it cooled and wondered if I should worry about that. I hoped not, and couldn't do anything about it anyway. I sat, limp and sweat-soaked in the control chair. The red warning light had gone back to yellow; the fault isolation had made sure the problem wasn't getting worse. Everything else was in the green. Exhausted, I slept.

∞ ∞ ∞

Two days later I had the nerve up for my next pass. By that time I'd missed the second set of asteroids and felt rather smug that I'd thought to set up a third.

I spent part of that time checking the guidescope. It turned out to be misaligned by less than 0.2 degrees —but whoever had calibrated it had misplaced a decimal and plugged in an almost two-degree "correction" factor. Somebody would hear about that.

I took another day to inspect the *Starfire* (maybe I *should* have named her *Argo*) after that first run. I suited up to check the hull exterior; remotes are fine, but I wanted to look for myself. The leading edges showed some abrasion, but nothing out of spec. A nickel-splashed dent the size of a dinner plate on the starboard fin confirmed my guess about the bang.

A chunk of the asteroid had wedged itself between rudder and fin, jamming the rudder. That had stalled the actuator and the already-hot motor immediately overheated. Fortunately it had shut itself off before the damage was permanent. I freed it up and got green lights on the board.

There was no structural damage, as far as I could tell, and I restored the fin contour by filling in the dent with thermal patch foam. I pondered writing Mitsubishi a letter of praise on their product, assuming I got out of this, but I wasn't sure they'd believe me.

When the hydrogen had been processed out of what I'd scooped, I had almost enough to get me to Procyon. It left me about a light-month short, but I could scoop that in a third the time of my previous run. Just as well, because I wasn't sure how much longer the compressor would last.

The smoke I thought I'd smelled worried me, so I tore panels off and examined all the electronics and cabling I could reach, but I didn't find any damage. Still, the cabin had been an oven on that first pass. I overrode the life support's climate control and set the temperature as low as it would go. By the time I started the second run my breath came in frosty clouds and I felt the cold in my fingers. Good.

Having done it once, the second run through BD-plus-five's atmosphere was slightly less terrifying. Slightly.

I played it conservatively, and there were no surprises. It got only sauna hot, but again it was exhausting. I was glad I didn't have to do it a third time.

∞ ∞ ∞

I was looking forward to an uneventful trip the rest of the way to Procyon. I carefully, oh so carefully lined it up in the now-recalibrated guidescope. I checked the spectrum three times. I checked the fuel calculations three times. I warped out of there, made my way back to my bunk, and fell asleep.

∞ ∞ ∞

"And you ended up here twenty hours later," Greg said. He'd heard I was on Procyon Station and came to find me, concerned because I'd been carried off the ship in a stretcher.

"Yeah. I set up the autopilot to slave to the station docking computer when it caught the beacon. Just as well, I was in no shape to do it manually." I waved my bandaged hands at him. I'd woken up in a bed in the infirmary, feeling like hell and with my extremities swaddled in surgical gauze. Greg had found me there.

"But why the bandages? Did you get burned, radiation or something?"

"No. Oh, I got a small dose of radiation, nothing serious." I didn't want to tell him, but he'd find out anyway. "I left the climate control turned down below freezing, I forgot to reset it. I got hypothermia. And frostbite."

The Sock Problem

"Honey, when are you going to fix the dryer?" my wife called from the laundry area.

I didn't answer right away. The clothes dryer had been acting up lately, emitting a god-awful buzzing when the start button was pushed and grudgingly coming up to speed if it started at all. The dryer was old, perhaps the bearings were worn.

"Honey? Did you hear me?"

"Yes sweetheart, I heard. I'll get started on it today." Appliance repair isn't rocket surgery. Open it up, figure out which part or parts are broken, and replace them. I even had the manual for this old Kenmore. The thing is, appliances are designed for easy assembly, not disassembly. Between hard-to-reach clips and ossified bolts, there are always skinned knuckles involved.

"While you're at it," my wife called again, "clean out the lint. Maybe you'll find some lost socks."

"Yes dear." Lint buildup was inevitable, and could be a fire hazard. It might even be causing the motor to overheat. The socks, though. . . .

Everyone jokes about socks disappearing from a dryer to leave unmatched singles. I only buy two kinds of socks, white athletic socks and black dress socks, in sufficient quantity that I never have a problem finding a match. I didn't know how often socks really disappeared from our dryer. Come to think of it, though, I bought more replacements than I discarded worn socks. Maybe they metamorphosed into wire coat hangers. No, that was paperclips.

∞ ∞ ∞

Disassembling the dryer cabinet proved easier than I'd expected. A couple of plastic clips held the lid down, and with the bolts undone the lid slid forward and up just fine. Aside from the control panel, no doubt redesigned every year to accommodate fashion and the latest five-cents-cheaper microcontroller, the innards of the dryer were surprisingly simple: a large steel drum to tumble the clothes, a heater for the intake air, a vent assembly, and a large motor with a pulley for the drum's belt drive. The air blower had its own motor, inefficient but unavoidable given the geometry.

I extracted the drum and cleaned out the felt-like layer of lint in the bottom of the cabinet. The drum motor was tucked away in the back corner.

It looked like a standard induction motor, with a labyrinth of wire coils that would have looked at home in a fusion reactor. Alternating current in the stator windings creates a moving magnetic field which induces a current in the rotor windings, and the changing electromagnetic fields turn the rotor. A starter coil helps overcome starting friction and inertia and get the motor up to speed.

Not in this case, though. My ohmmeter showed the starter switch was within spec, but I got intermittent readings on the resistance of the motor coils.

I plugged the dryer back in and, against all the warnings in the manual, tested it with the cabinet open so I could watch the motor. Sure enough, sometimes it would start almost immediately, but often it would emit a raucous buzz while the rotor crept around like a clock's second hand.

Rewinding a motor with that coil geometry wasn't something I wanted to tackle. I'd have to replace it. There was a Sears repair and parts center only a few miles away.

∞ ∞ ∞

"I'm going to the parts place to pick up a new motor," I called to my wife.

"Can I come?" That was my son Isaac, always eager to go somewhere new.

In the car, he was as talkative as only a preteen can be. "So the dryer needs a motor? Is it broken? Did you find out where the socks went?"

"Whoa, slow down. In order: yes; mostly yes; and what socks?"

"You know, how we're always losing single socks from a pair in the dryer. Do they get sucked out the vent?"

"No, there's a grille. Nothing bigger than a pea is going out the vent."

"So maybe the socks shrink really tiny." Isaac has quite an imagination.

"No, I think they go through a space warp." This was a game we sometimes played, coming up with outlandish explanations.

"Why not a time warp?"

"Okay, a spacetime warp. It's formed by the interaction of the complicated magnetic field from the motor, and the rotation of the drum. The metal drum picks up an induced field and right in the center, a spacetime vortex forms. Any sock falling through it disappears." I was proud of that one, it almost made sense.

"So why don't other clothes disappear?" Isaac asked.

"Um, they're too big. They fall off the baffles too soon so don't get close enough to the vortex."

"Underwear is small."

I had to think about that one for a bit. Then I had it. "Maybe it's the topology of the—"

"Topology? You mean like how a donut is like a coffee mug, they both have one hole that goes all the way through?" Isaac reads a lot for middle school.

"Exactly. Most clothing, except socks, has arm holes or leg holes. Maybe that creates a weak circuit that interferes with the vortex. Socks don't."

"That explains why I never lose a sock that has a hole in it!" He paused. "Hey! Maybe the missing socks splat like bugs on the window of Dr. Who's TARDIS!"

I laughed out loud at that one.

∞ ∞ ∞

Back at home with a new motor I began to reassemble everything. I pulled the pulley from the old motor and attached it to the new. Replacing the motor in its housing I only skinned my knuckles once. A couple of quick tests confirmed that it started almost instantly, a vast improvement. I put the rest of it back together.

Before closing the lid I did one more test to make sure everything was seated properly. I pushed the button, the motor started up and the drum started turning happily . . . the wrong way.

Damn, I must have installed the new motor backwards. It had a different starter switch and wiring harness, and I hadn't realized. I inspected the drum mounting, the belt and idler wheels, and confirmed that the airflow, thanks to the separate motor, was still correct. The dryer should still work as a dryer.

I ran a load of laundry. Even with the motor swapped end for end and the drum turning in reverse, the dryer worked fine.

Only now, more and more, we keep finding *extra* socks.

Author's Note

This was an invited story for the *Full-Throttle Space Tales* volume, *Space Horrors*. I had fun writing it (but then, I have fun writing most of my stories.) Fans of Edgar Allan Poe will recognize my inspiration. I confess that the horrible pun in the title was intentional.

Poetic Justice

The sleeper ship *Raven* sliced the icy, inky trans-Plutonian darkness a light-year out from Earth.

"Come on, Trevor, old man, you've had plenty of sleep, two years in fact. Time to wake up." Joe Fontano's voice carried a note of forced cheerfulness.

Trevor Montgomery heard and resented the words. He resented being woken up, and resented the cheery tone when he felt like death warmed over. Hibernation wasn't supposed to be like this. He felt as though he'd had a tormented night's sleep instead of waking up alert. It ought to be as though he'd just laid down. He opened his eyes, then squinted against the glare. "Turn those accursed lights down!"

"They are. It's dark in here, you're just used to it. But I have to do this." Fontano held up a small flashlight and shone it in Trevor's eyes; first the right, then the left.

"Ow, damn you!" It felt like a laser.

"Sorry. Your pupil response is good."

Trevor blinked away the after-image of the flashlight. He looked around. Yes, the hibernation vault did have an almost Stygian gloom to it, now.

Fontano gestured at the multi-colored graph on the nearby display. "Your vitals are okay. You don't have freezer burn."

"Freezer burn? I was not supposed to be frozen." Trevor scowled. The hibernaculums were supposed to maintain body temperature at four degrees Celsius, well above where ice crystals could form. He'd helped design them himself.

"That was a joke. Lighten up, you're the first live human I've had a conversation with in months." Fontano suddenly smiled. "Hey, at least I didn't tell you to chill out."

Trevor scowled again. Fontano was ill-suited for this work, always playing the fool, never taking things seriously. How had he managed to stay sane those months alone? He himself had that to look forward to now.

The *Raven*, like all sleeper ships, carried its hundred passengers and dozen crew members in cold sleep. This artificial hibernation reduced life support requirements to something manageable for the decade-long trip between stars. In rotation, each crew member would take a turn awake for six months at a time to oversee the ship's systems, then revive his replacement. The ship's life support reserves allowed a week of overlap with the two of them awake, to ensure no after-effects from the hibernation and to provide time for the shift hand-off.

Trevor examined the display of his vital signs. Fontano had been correct about them looking normal, but that was only the present status. "My head aches, it's throbbing. Are you sure my blood oxygen was normal?"

"If you can trust the sensors." Fontano said, and grinned. Trevor had designed them. "I was okay when I came out of hibernation—" he broke off and coughed. "Well, except for the cough. Must have been the cold and the dry air."

Trevor glared at him. The humidity in the hibernaculums was controlled. "Cold temperatures won't
give you a cough, not unless they didn't sterilize everything properly." But Fontano did look a bit pallid.

"Whatever. Look, let's get you up. Can you sit up?
Get out of that thing?" Trevor sat up slowly. He
didn't feel the strain he had expected. The ship's
"gravity" was artificial, the result of constant acceleration at one-tenth of Earth-normal gravity. The problem with standing was balance, not strength, but he
soon adapted to it.

"Well done!" Fontano applauded briefly. "We'll
have you doing cartwheels down the corridors in no
time."

Trevor looked forward to the end of the week; to
when he would put Fontano and his abrasive manners
and loud-mouthed humor into hibernation; to when
he would have the ship blissfully to himself.

∞ ∞ ∞

The following days dragged wearily on.

"The way I see it, Trevor, is that with two of us
awake we only need to do half the work each. We can
split the tasks."

"Your math is impeccable, of course," said
Trevor, his hint of sarcasm lost on Fontano. "But to
what end? I need to review all the ship's systems, and
you are supposed to check that I sill remember how
after my time in hibernation. Although I will grant
you that the latter task is hardly necessary."

"Of course it's not necessary. Oh, I'll double
check you on today's work, but the rest of the
week. . .pfah." Fontano waved a hand airily. "Then we

can have more free time together. We can talk, or play games. I have a deck of cards."

Trevor shuddered. "Why, that would be delightful." It would not, but he could tolerate it for a week. "But first we must get our work done. Where are you in the inspection rotation?"

The inspection of the ship's systems was largely make-work, something to keep the awake crew member busy. The ship's internal sensors and self-diagnostic routines should discover any problems before a manual inspection would. Human attention should only be needed if something actually needed replacement or repair. But the inspection routines kept the crew's skills honed, and there was always a chance that a fault could arise in the fault-detection systems themselves. If a serious problem developed, additional crew could be revived from hibernation to assist.

"The top floor," said Fontano.

"Top floor?" The phrasing was unfamiliar to Trevor.

"You know, all the way forward. Under acceleration that's 'up', so the top floor. Then there's the forward deuterium tanks, the middle floors are the wardroom and bridge. The hibernation vaults are the cellar. Cargo and aft tanks in the sub-basement and engines in the sub-sub-basement." Fontano grinned. "See, it makes perfect sense."

"I do see. Did you devise this nomenclature or was it something you inherited from Lucerne?" Roger Lucerne had preceded Fontano in the awake rotation.

"Pfah! Lucerne is an ignoramus. He's got no imagination. I came up with it." Fontano beamed.

"Ah, well then. By all means, let us proceed to the top floor and begin our inspection."

∞ ∞ ∞

By the fourth day, Trevor estimated that he'd suffered through a thousand of Fontano's stupid little jokes or half-witty sayings. He didn't know which was worse: performing all the inspections with Fontano double-checking him, as per procedure; or splitting the inspection work between the two of them, leaving that much more unassigned time during each day. Trevor would have been perfectly content using that time to work his way through the ship's extensive library of books and videos, but Fontano was always yammering on about something, or telling stupid jokes. Knowing that it was temporary, Trevor bore this as best he could. But sometimes he had to get away.

"I'm going down to the cellar to inspect the hibernaculums." Trevor said, tossing his handful of cards on the wardroom table as he got up.

Fontano looked up from his own hand. "Your hand is that bad, eh? Ha, ha, ugh!" His laugh turned into coughing. He caught his breath and began to gather up the pile of cards on the table. "We already did that inspection. Are you losing your memory?"

Trevor shook his head. "No, we did the standard inspection. That's all very well as far as it goes, but you'll recall that I helped to design these hibernation chambers. I just want to do a more detailed inspection, to satisfy my own curiosity. No, don't get up, I don't need any help."

Fontano shrugged. "Alright, suit yourself. The damn cold makes my cough worse anyway. Ha, 'suit', and we were playing cards. Get it?" He started to lay the cards out on the table for solitaire.

Trevor rolled his eyes as he walked from the wardroom.

∞ ∞ ∞

It was cold and gloomy in the hibernation vaults. The hibernaculums themselves were individually re-frigerated, but the vault itself was kept cool and dark; there was no point in wasting energy. Trevor had no intention of examining every one of the chambers, he would just do a few at random. But there was one in particular that he intended to check.

He located the hibernaculum and looked long-ingly through the transparent cover at the figure within. Even in cold sleep she was radiant. He touched a display panel and it lit up, displaying a brief status report and the occupant's name: Eleanor Mont-gomery.

Working with precise movements, Trevor Mont-gomery removed the screws from a service panel cover and then set the cover on the deck. Revealed within the hibernaculum's machinery, amidst an or-derly array of wires and plastic tubes, was the system's master control processor. Trevor took a small hand-held computer from one pocket and a cable from the other, then used the cable to connect the hand-held to the port on the hibernaculum's processor.

He spent several minutes reviewing data on the hand-held's display, periodically punching in com-mands and reading the results. He began to mutter under his breath. Finally, deliberately, he unplugged the cable and replaced the panel cover, muttering all the while.

He stood up and turned to look around the vault. It was as gloomy and quiet as it had been earlier. He turned back to the casket he'd been working on, and gazed once more upon Eleanor. He clenched a fist. "I will have my revenge."

∞ ∞ ∞

"Fontano, you're scheduled for hibernation today." Trevor stepped into the ward room and held up a small device; a hypospray. "Your sedative."

"Already? I'm starting to enjoy this. You know they made a mistake, planning for only one person awake at a time. The time goes so much more quickly with two."

Was he insane? "Well, but that would put twice the drain on the ship's life support, we would run out of consumables."

"Oh, I know that. It's just. . ." his voice trailed off.

"You don't want to go back into hibernation?"

"It's cold. The hibernaculums are like coffins." He stared off at nothing. He coughed his annoying cough again, then he turned and grinned. "Still, I guess I won't die of sleep, eh?"

"No, Fontano, I promise you won't die of sleep."

"I just worry that I'll dream." He held up a hand to forestall Trevor's interruption. "No, I didn't last time. But, my next shift is in five years. Can you imagine, lying there dreaming all that time? Or worse, having nightmares?"

"Nonsense, you won't know a thing. You will be

in suspended animation, you know that." Trevor paused, as if considering. "I'll tell you what, though. I can give you a stronger shot of sedative before prepping you for hibernation. You'll be out before you go under." Trevor held up the hypospray and twisted a dial on it, increasing the dose.

Fontano looked relieved. "Yes, I'm just a little nervous about going back under."

"Not to worry. Although you're the expert." He held the hypospray ready.

"What? You know far more about the hibernation systems than I do."

"I merely meant that you've already put someone under on this trip. I have only done it in the lab," Trevor said as the injector hissed its contents into Fontano's arm.

"What? Oh, yes, right. I thought you meant something else."

"That you revived Eleanor for a few weeks and put her back under too? Yes, there is that."

Fontano's eyes widened in surprise, then his eyes rolled back and he slumped to the deck, unconscious.

"Yes, there is indeed that," said Trevor coldly. He picked Fontano up, not a great burden in the *Raven*'s low acceleration gravity, and carried him down to the hibernation vaults in the "cellar".

∞ ∞ ∞

Fontano awoke while Trevor was prepping the hibernation chamber. *Good*, Trevor had judged the dosage properly.

Fontano looked about himself wildly, looked up through the transparent cover of the hibernaculum, and struggled briefly against the straps holding him in place. He groped for the strap release button but there was only a hole in the plastic where the button should be.

"Trevor, you? What?"

"Ah, you're awake. How fortunate."

"But, what is going on? Is my hibernation over? What happened to Lucerne, why are *you* waking me up?"

"Oh no, your hibernation has not begun."

"What? But. . . . But the straps!"

"Ah, yes. I had to remove the release button. My apologies for not doing a neater job and covering that hole, but I might want to replace the button later. After you're asleep."

Fontano squirmed then relaxed. Slowly a look of comprehension crept over his face, and he struggled again. "Trevor! What you said before, about Eleanor, that's crazy!"

"Is it? You hid the signs well enough. Nothing in the main logs, nothing on the ship's internal monitors."

"That's because nothing happened! Let me out of here and let's talk about this."

"Oh no, I cannot let you out. It is time for your hibernation. Besides, there is nothing to talk about. I know that you are very good with computers, no doubt you edited the logs. Most of them, anyway."

"I didn't touch the logs. What are you talking about?"

"Please don't insult my intelligence. Did you think I wouldn't check the detailed logs on my own wife's hibernaculum? Was it she who told you to modify

that log too?" Trevor held up a screwdriver to show
Fontano. The other hand held the service panel cover
for a hibernation chamber.

"What are you talking about?"

"The internal event log in the control unit. Each
chamber has its own processors, and they talk to the
ship's computers." He waved the panel cover. "Not
that you can see it from where you lie, but this one is
from yours, by the way."

A shiver ran through Fontano. "I don't know
what you're talking about. I never touched Eleanor's
hibernaculum, or any logs."

"Then why did the event log show a reset?"
Trevor shook his head. "You thought you had wiped
the memory so it would appear to be a glitch, but I
went digging into the backup memory. You revived
her because you wanted company. Was she a willing
accomplice or did you force yourself on her?"

Fontano shook his head wildly. "That's crazy talk.
Yes, there was a power glitch, that's in the ship's main
log too. But I didn't revive anybody! I don't know
what you saw in the backup memory, maybe a ghost
image, bad data. Let me out and we'll check out the
other systems."

Trevor had been bent over the internals of the hibernation unit as Fontano talked. He stood up and
looked at Fontano. "An amusing story. Now let me
tell you one. What I'm doing here," he said as he
turned back to the service panel, "is reprogramming
your hibernaculum."

"Reprogramming?" There was an edge of hysteria
to Fontano's voice.

"Yes. I'm afraid you won't be going to sleep before the temperature in there starts dropping. In fact —" he paused to make a delicate adjustment. "In fact, you won't be going to sleep for quite a while. I gave you a stimulant to wake you up just now, and the hibernation chamber will maintain that. You might be awake for days. Of course, I had to flush the Hybernazine reservoir."

"Trevor! You can't do that!"

"Oh, don't worry about the life support reserves. Your little glass casket there will drop the temperature and oxygen levels just as though you were hibernating. The rest of the ship will be fine."

"No!"

"No? You're probably right, you probably won't be awake for days. Once the hypothermia and hypoxia sets in, you'll go right to sleep." He replaced the cover on the service panel and began tightening its screws. "But don't worry, you won't dream."

"For the love of God, Trevor!" Fontano struggled again against the straps, squirming violently on the bed of the hibernaculum.

"Yes," Trevor said, "for the love, anyway." He secured the last screw then switched off the interior light on the hibernaculum. He turned to leave the hibernaculum storage area. At the vault door he paused. He could still hear, although faintly, the sounds of Fontano's struggles and screams for help.

Trevor shook his head. *A loudmouth to the last.* He closed the door and latched it.

Author's Note

Alpha Centauri: First Landing is actually the third T-Space novel I wrote, after *The Chara Talisman* and *The Reticuli Deception*, but it is (as you might guess from the title) the earliest chronologically.

To date it is my most popular book, and it sells relatively well in Australia. Sometimes I wonder if that's because you can actually *see* Alpha Centauri from there.

Excerpt from the Novel

Alpha Centauri: First Landing

Chapter 1: A Change of Plans

Commodore Drake's office, Centauri Mission HQ, Earth

"No I do *not* want that man on the mission!" Elizabeth Sawyer all but shouted. "He's an egotistical, sloppy, stubborn, irreverent . . . jerk!" Then, obviously remembering she was talking to her commanding officer, added: "Sir."

Commodore Franklin Drake took a deep breath and let it out slowly. "Look, Elizabeth, I know he's your ex. I know you guys had some, uh, interesting screaming matches. But with Doctor Grainger out of commission, we need a well-qualified exobiologist. George Darwin has the expertise and space experience. I know you're both intelligent enough to be able to get along. It's not like you ever came to blows."

Sawyer's smile tightened. "I'd have kicked his butt if it had."

Drake had no doubt of that. Commander Elizabeth Sawyer was a powerfully-built woman, with years of field geology under her belt before her astronaut training.

"What about Wallace?" Sawyer continued. "Can we get him back? And who let Grainger's backup go this close to the Centauri mission launch anyway?"

Drake shook his head. "Politics. When Wallace heard about possible lifeforms under the ice on Enceladus, there was no holding him back. He pulled strings to get on the next mission. I'm sure he'd much rather go to Alpha Centauri but it didn't look like that was going to happen. Our international partners had no problem with it, of course—"

Sawyer snorted. "Not if they had a chance for one of their own to do the first footstep if something happened to Grainger." She paused a moment. "It *was* an accident, right?"

The thought startled Drake. There *had* been plenty of political bickering over who would be first to set foot on an extrasolar planet, but it was the United States who had developed a workable warp drive. It had also been an American robotic probe which returned from Alpha Centauri with images of not one, but *two* Earth-like planets in that system, apparently complete with life forms. The partners had agreed to let an American take the first footstep on whichever of those they landed. It was also agreed that should be an exobiologist. But now Grainger's backup was on his way to Saturn, and the next most qualified exobiologist was either European or Chinese. There might be some motive to arrange an accident. Still, Drake couldn't bring himself to believe anyone with access would stoop to that.

"Yeah, almost certainly. Of course it's being investigated, just like any other on the job accident. Anyway, George Darwin has been designated as second backup all along."

"But he's in charge of the Lunar Quarantine Lab. People who don't know George like I do might think he'd prefer that to doing the first footsteps. He's had his fame and glory, and he's the boss of the facility that will be first to get its hands on whatever alien specimens the Centauri mission brings back. I can just imagine some Eurocrat thinking that's a preferred position to being stuck in a tin can for up to six months." Sawyer shook her head again. "Gods, I don't want to be cooped up with that man for that long."

"You know you won't be. A week to Alpha Centauri, a couple of weeks of preliminary survey, then he'll be down planet-side until it's time to return. Everyone's going to be busy." Drake could tell that she wasn't convinced. He knew they could handle it; they had on the Mars mission, which had been longer. Under any other circumstances, Elizabeth Sawyer was one of the most even-tempered people he knew. But there was one other point.

"Sawyer," he said, "it's out of my hands. The higher ups insist on Darwin. If you don't think you can handle it . . . well, you have a backup too."

Her eyes flared, and she slammed her palm on his desk. "No! I will not be bumped from the mission because of that man." She settled back in her seat. "We'll be fine, on our best behavior." She muttered something else, which Drake didn't quite catch, but it might have been "or I'll break his arm."

"All right. I'm counting on both of you not to let me down." Drake made some notations on his computer. He should break this to Darwin in person, to make sure he got the whole message too. He would have to review his task list, to see what else could he get done while on Luna. But first. . . .

"Speaking of crew assignments," he said, "how are we coming on plans to redistribute the European contingent amongst the remaining ships?"

"So we're not waiting on the *Jules Verne*? I can't say I'm sorry."

The European ship, the *Jules Verne*, had run into problems during its interplanetary shakedown testing. Waiting for repairs would push the mission back several months.

"No. Our taxpayers don't want to wait, and the Chinese, Russians and Indians aren't willing to either. Their ships are ready. The *Verne* is to be held in reserve. Maybe they'll send it out if we're not back in six months, but some of the crew comes with us."

"Okay. At least they didn't name it the *Perry Rhodan*."

Drake snorted. For a while, that had looked like a real possibility, because of a popular campaign. Just as *his* ship had almost been named the *USS Enterprise* instead of the *USS Robert A. Heinlein*.

Chapter 2: The Moon

Interstellar Quarantine Facility, on the Moon

Drake finished suiting up for the walk from the lander to the base itself. At any other base on the Moon, there would be a docking tunnel or some other convenient way of getting from the ship to the buildings without going outside. Here, though, the short trip outside was part of the quarantine protocol. If something got loose in the lab, it would be that much harder for it to get back to Earth.

It was also a pain in the ass.

He exited the airlock and bounced along the surface to the lab. At least they'd hardened it—"paved" wasn't quite the word, it had been sintered using focused sunlight—so he wasn't kicking up dust at every step like the first time he'd set foot on the Moon. How many years ago had that been? Too many.

He was expected, of course, and some minor assistant was there to help him out of his suit as he cleared the lab entrance.

"Welcome to the Moon. We weren't given details of your visit, just that you were arriving. What can we do for you?"

"Later I'll want a tour of the facility, I expect to be spending some time here when we get back from our mission."

"Of course, sir. Um, you said later? Was there something first?"

"I want to pay a visit to an old friend. Where's Darwin's office? I'll find my own way."

"Uh, Director Darwin is a busy man—"

"So am I, and I outrank him. I also want to surprise him. Now, which way?" Drake felt a little bad about taking that tone, but what was the point of having rank if you couldn't pull it once in a while? The aide gave him the directions and he set off down the high-ceilinged corridor.

∞ ∞ ∞

Darwin's office

"You've gained weight since Mars, George." Drake said.

Darwin looked up from his desk, scowling. Then he recognized the unexpected visitor at his door and smiled. "Captain Drake! I didn't know you'd arrived, I'll have to talk to someone about that. Come in. What brings you here?"

Drake entered the office and seated himself in the chair across the desk from Darwin. "It's Commodore Drake now, actually. Commanding a fleet and all that, if a small one." He paused a moment, glancing around the high-ceilinged office, taking in the spider plants hanging in the corner, the pictures on the wall. Most were scenes from Earth, of Darwin in unusual environments. Hot springs, a glacier. He recognized one, a bleak rocky landscape in shades of red with a pinkish sky. Two space-suited figures posed for the picture; Darwin and himself. "You have *that* picture on your wall? I get tired of seeing it."

Darwin glanced over his shoulder at it. "That's why it's behind me. It's to impress visitors, my glory days."

"Don't say that, it makes you sound like an old man, and where does that leave me?"

"In my office trying to avoid telling me why you're here when I thought you had a starship to make ready."

"You're right," Drake said. "Neither of us was ever much for small talk. How would you like to go to Alpha Centauri?"

The look on Darwin's face was almost worth the trip in itself. It managed to combine deer-in-the-head-lights with complete disbelief with a kid seeing the presents under the tree on Christmas morning.

"What? In what capacity? You've got an exobiologist."

Drake shook his head. "Actually we don't. Grainger managed to fall off the descent ladder in a rehearsal exercise. He broke some bones and punctured his spleen. He's not going."

"Is he all right? No, stupid question."

"He's fixable, but waiting for him would push back the schedule, and our international partners don't want to wait. China and the European Union have already offered replacement exobiologists."

"Hah, no way that's going to happen." The first ship to land would be the Indian vessel *Subrahmanyan*

Chandrasekhar, but the privilege of first footstep would go to the mission's lead exobiologist. "But what about Grainger's backup?"

"Wallace? Last month the Enceladus exploration team found signs of life under the ice. Since it looked like he wouldn't be needed on the Centauri mission he lit out for Saturn as soon as he could get authorization. We could get him back—Saturn is at least on the same side of the Sun as we're going, although we're headed out of the ecliptic—but I decided to offer the slot to you first. I know it's a bit of a demotion, but —"

"No, no. I mean, sure, I'd have to give up the glamour and excitement of running the Interstellar Quarantine Lab, but I'm willing to sacrifice to help out an old friend."

Drake snorted. "Right. The opportunity to investigate two planets' worth of alien lifeforms first hand has nothing to do with it."

Darwin smiled. "Well, maybe a little." He sat forward on his seat, sobering. "Okay, how long do I have to transfer operation of this lab, and what's my training schedule going to be?"

Drake wasn't surprised at how quickly Darwin had gotten down to business. It was one of the things he liked about him. He pulled a data chip from his pocket and placed it on the desk in front of Darwin. "The details are all in there. You already have plenty of space experience, and you're one of the best exobiologists in the business, so your focus will be the detailed mission plan—"

"Okay, I know some of that from how it ties into the LQL requirements for when you, or we, get back. And I developed the mission biology protocols."

"I know. The only other thing is general starship systems, although aside from the warp drive it's not much different from what we went to Mars in."

"Oh, and about that," Darwin said.

"Yes?"

"The gravity is lower here. I've *lost* weight since Mars."

Drake laughed and shook his head. "All right. Read through the briefing on the chip and contact me later today." He turned to leave, then stopped and turned back. "There is one other thing."

"What's that?"

"Elizabeth Sawyer is on the mission team. Will that be a problem?"

The deer-in-the-headlights look came back, this time without being combined with the kid on Christmas morning. So much for being happy to see her again, Drake thought.

"In what capacity?"

"My second in command, and geologist. Look, I know you two can get along in public. And for all the screaming matches, it never got physical, right?"

A wry grin crept onto Darwin's face, like he was remembering something. "Well, not in *that* sense. She'd have broken my arm."

Drake remembered something he'd once heard about makeup sex being the best kind. Fortunately his dark skin didn't show a blush. "I don't need to know any other details. So, no problem?"

Darwin's expression sobered. He looked a little like he'd swallowed a bug, but said: "No, no problem at all."

∞ ∞ ∞

One problem down, a dozen to go, Drake mused as he left the quarantine lab. The planned six-ship fleet was already down to five, after the problems with the European craft *Jules Verne*, leaving him to rearrange the crew to ensure a European presence, and ever since the robotic probe, Nessus, had returned with pictures of not just one, but two Earth like planets in the Centauri system, the taxpayers were anxious to see a mission get out there and "boldly go where no-one had gone before".

More importantly, at least to the United States government, was the concern that China and perhaps other nations were close to discovering the secret to creating a stable warp field. Without warp technology to bargain with, the Chinese-designed compact tokamak fusion reactors necessary for a manned warp ship might suddenly become unavailable, giving China a monopoly on interstellar flight. The fission reactors that powered the Nessus put out too much radiation to be used within the limited confines of a warp bubble with humans present, and their relatively limited power reduced both the size of that bubble and the available speed. Not a problem for a robotic probe, but unworkable for sending a crew beyond the solar system.

Politics. Drake hadn't gotten where he was by ignoring it, but that didn't mean he liked it.

Chapter 3: Geologists

Centauri Mission Headquarters, Earth

Sawyer's omniphone beeped at her. She glanced at the screen on her wrist, it was reminding her of a meeting with Fred Tyrell, another of the geology crew. *Already ahead of you*, she thought, as she entered Tyrell's office.

"So, Fred, anything new?" The man before her had the characteristic leathery skin of someone who had spent more time in the field than in the classroom or laboratory.

"I've been going over the geology manifest. With the extra crew member our mass allotment has been cut by over a hundred kilos. That seems excessive, especially considering that the biology team has been similarly cut."

"It's not just the mass of the crew member. We're adding a couch and life support reserves. I know it sucks, but it's what we've got."

Fred sighed. "Yeah, I realize that. At least we're not totally eliminating any of the experiment packages, just reducing the redundancy somewhat. For example, we're only taking half the geophones and seismic charges you wanted to."

That would cut into their ability to do detailed subsurface profiling, and who knew what interesting clues to the planetary history. "That's unfortunate. What about the ANT gear?" That would give them a gross picture of the planetary interiors, but nothing fine grained.

"No change there. The neutrino detectors are built into the ship. Even if we wanted to take them out it would delay things too much. As long as we have a working reactor to generate anti-neutrinos, we're good."

"And if we don't, we have bigger problems," Sawyer said. "What else?"

"What do you think of cutting the equipment on the fliers? There's a lot of sensor gear there. If we cut out either the multispectral scanner or the ground imaging radar that's a good percent of our weight right there."

Sawyer considered this. The fliers were electric ultralight aircraft, powered by photovoltaic film in the wings, and modified from a commercially available model to fold up for storage in the lander. She hated to lose any of the sensor gear. "If we take out one of those, could we rig the flier for an extra passenger? Might come in handy."

Fred's brow furrowed as he thought about it. "It'd be heavier with three people, but it might be workable. We want to make sure we have margin. The radar is heavier, and the biologists will care more about the multispectral anyway."

Personally Sawyer cared more about the ground radar. Overlying vegetation, which the radar could see through, often hid interesting geophysical details. But the multispectral scanner could also reveal things about surface chemistry. And it didn't hurt to keep the biologists happy—she winced as she remembered who the new lead biologist was—it was the fact that there were clear signs of life in the Alpha Centauri system that was driving the mission, after all. "Okay," she said, "let's do the biologists a favor."

"Speaking of biologists, I have a training session with them tomorrow. We're going on a field trip."

"You're teaching them geology?"

"Yes and no. Surprisingly, there's not a paleontologist in the bunch."

"But I thought—"

"Oh, sure, they know some, especially in their own specialties, but no field paleontologists. They want me to show them what to look for in terms of possible fossil-bearing formations. Actually, I think they wanted you, but you've got your hands full."

"Tell me about it. So what did you have in mind?"

"A couple of ten- or fifteen-kilometer hikes through some interesting formations. I'm limiting it to what's most likely to be in range of the landing areas, so nothing too arctic." Orbital mechanics meant keeping the landings away from the poles to maximize their payload.

"Okay. By the way, I don't know when he's due Earth-side, he may already be back, but George Darwin is now leading the biology team. He's Grainger's replacement. If he's back he'll be joining your field trips, he needs time with his team."

"Darwin?" Tyrell's expression suggested that he wanted to add some comment but wasn't sure if he should. He settled for saying: "He's been on the Moon for what, several months now? He won't have his Earth legs back yet. I'll go easy on him."

"Don't." At Tyrell's startled look, she realized that had sounded more mean-spirited than she'd intended. "The planets we're going to are Earth sized, and we'll be spending two weeks or so in zero gee before we get there. He's going to need to rebuild his muscles before that. He'd tell you the same thing." Knowing Darwin's stubborn pride, she had no doubt of that.

Tyrell still seemed skeptical, but nodded. "All right. I hope for his sake he's been keeping up his exercise program."

"He was a fanatic about it on the way to Mars. The man's a born overachiever."

"And you're not?" Fred said, then looked down and mumbled "Sorry".

Sawyer wasn't offended. "Yes, I guess I am. That's probably why we got along so well," she with a wry smile.

Chapter 4: Field Trip

Geology Field Training Site 1, Earth

Fred Tyrell surveyed his troupe of biologists, who stood looking expectantly at him in the morning sun. He waited as the rotor throb of their helicopter faded in the distance. He'd met all of them before at various training and orientation sessions, of course, but except for the American crew, he didn't know any of them well.

There was Dr. Jennifer Singh—they all had at least doctorates in one field or another—the botanist, part of the Indian contingent. George Darwin, of course, who didn't seem in the least perturbed standing there in gravity six times what he'd been living in for the last few months. *We'll see how long that lasts*, thought Fred. Dr. Xiaojing Wu, the Chinese microbiologist. Then there was Dr. Ulrika Klaar, whose picture could be in the dictionary beside the definition of "Nordic beauty". Tall, with long, straight, almost platinum blonde hair which normally hung loose to her waist but now was done up in a more sensible braid. Fred wondered if she'd get it cut before the mission left; long hair could be a hassle in zero gee.

It hadn't occurred to Fred before, but looking out over the team he realized the disproportionate representation of females in the biology team. He shrugged. Nothing wrong with that.

"All right people, listen up," he said. "We're going to head north for about eight kilometers to where the chopper will be waiting to take us to the next site. It's not a race but it would be nice to be there in time for lunch. We'll be traversing a mix of rock types, from sedimentary to igneous—" Dr. Singh coughed and raised her hand.

"Yes?"

"Why igneous? Surely there would not be any fossils in igneous rocks?"

"In general you'd be correct." At least somebody was paying attention. "We certainly wouldn't find fossils in granites or basalts, although it helps to know what isn't biologically of interest too. However a lava flow or volcanic ash-fall can preserve larger structures like trees, or footprints, and I'm sure George or Xiaojing could tell you all about microfossils near hot springs."

"Of course, thank you."

"No worries. If anyone has questions, just call them out, let's keep this informal."

He checked the map on his omniphone, looked up at the sun as though to confirm his sense of direction, and gestured toward a low hill a few hundred meters away. "All right, let's head out that way." He began lecturing as they hiked. "What we're walking on is shale, where it shows between the vegetation. It's a layered stone, made from mud and clay, with a lot more silicate than your limestone, and where it does show fossils they can show a lot of fine detail . . ." Fred had given lectures like this often enough that he could probably do them in his sleep. It occurred to him that they wouldn't be relying on their omni-phones much on the planets of Alpha Centauri. They'd have satellite photos and some location infor-mation from the ships that remained in orbit, but nothing like the network of navigation satellites which girdled Earth. Perhaps he should throw in a lesson on reading a compass. At least the planets they were going to had magnetic fields.

Chapter 5: Departure

Interstellar Quarantine Facility, on the Moon

"Director Darwin, I wasn't sure we'd be seeing you before you returned from Alpha Centauri."

"That's ex-Director now, Doctor Kemmerer is the Director."

"Of course. It was a courtesy title. So, one last look around before heading off into deep space?"

"Something like that. Does Charles know I'm here?"

"He does. He had planned to meet you here himself but got called away at the last moment. He said he'd be back as soon as he could."

Darwin sighed. "I know how that goes."

At that moment Charles Kemmerer came in through the hatchway leading to the rest of the base. "George, welcome back. Sorry about not being here in person," he said, shaking Darwin's hand.

"No worries. And I'm not here to jog your elbow. Mostly just give the place a once-over, and to congratulate you."

"Congratulate me? On what?"

"You're no longer Acting Director, you're confirmed as the full Director of this place. I can't have two jobs at once, so my resignation as Director here has been accepted, I'm now the 'Director of Field Exobiology for the Alpha Centauri Expedition'."

"Well, thank you, and congratulations to you too. And you're welcome to it. This is about as far as I want to get from Earth," Kemmerer said.

"Ha! Fair enough. So, shall we go say hello to a few folks? And if you have any questions, now's your last chance to ask them."

With that, the two left the reception area and headed down a hallway in an easy low-gravity loping walk. Darwin had to watch his step. His month on Earth had altered his muscles and reflexes, but the method came back to him, like riding a bicycle.

Kemmerer picked up the conversation. "I was your deputy for six months, I probably know where more bodies are buried than you do," he said, and grinned. "But how long do you have? When we heard you were coming, some of the gang wanted to throw you a bon voyage party."

Darwin smiled at that. "I'll be back here in a couple of months, albeit as an inmate rather than Director—"

"Guest," Kemmerer interrupted, "or perhaps at worst patient. Inmate sounds a bit . . . depressing."

"Guest, then. I need to leave tomorrow to rendezvous with the *Heinlein* and the rest of the fleet, but sure, I'm up for something informal this evening."

∞ ∞ ∞

The going away party was indeed small and informal, as Darwin had hoped. The staffing level at the facility would rise when the Centauri crew was due to return, and many of the technicians involved in the construction had already departed, so what was left was a small maintenance crew of technicians and biologists to maintain the samples they'd be testing for exposure to anything brought back from Alpha Centauri. It was similar to what had been done for the first few Apollo Moon landings a century earlier.

Toward the end of the party, Kemmerer produced a small gift-wrapped package and handed it to Darwin.

"What's this?" Darwin asked, taking the package.

"Go ahead and open it. It's too late for your Mars trip, not that you needed it, and we hope you don't need it at Alpha Centauri either."

Puzzled, Darwin shook the package gently. It didn't rattle or make any noise, and whatever was inside felt moderately dense. He had no idea. He tore the wrapping off and opened the small specimen box inside, then laughed.

"A *potato*?"

"Yes, *Solanum tuberosum*. We had extras."

Darwin grinned and held it up for the others to see. "Thank you all. I may have briefly been a Martian, but I'm no Mark Watney. Let's hope I don't need this."

That drew a round of applause and congratulations.

A short while later Darwin bid everyone his good-byes and retired to his room. He'd be leaving first thing in the morning.

∞ ∞ ∞

The story continues in Alpha Centauri: First Landing, *available now in e-book and trade paperback.*

Mabash Books by Alastair Mayer

Early T-Space: The Alpha Centauri Series

Alpha Centauri: First Landing
Alpha Centauri: Sawyer's World
Alpha Centauri: The Return

coming soon:
Alpha Centauri: Kakuloa

The Carson & Roberts Series:
Archeological adventures in T-Space

The Chara Talisman
The Reticuli Deception
The Eridani Convergence

coming soon:
The Pavonis Insurgence